PROM
IN THE

Mattisyn Elizabeth

Copyright © 2023 Mattisyn Elizabeth
Identity Light Publishing

All rights reserved. No part of this book may be reproduced or used in any manner without written permission of the copyright owner except for the use of quotations in a book review.

For more information or permissions, contact:
copyright@idlpublishing.com

ISBN: 979-8-218-95651-6 (paperback)

This is a work of fiction. Names, characters, places, and incidents either are the product of the author's imagination or are used fictitiously. Any resemblance to actual persons, living or dead, events, or locales is entirely coincidental.

First paperback edition June 2023

Book design by Ashley DeCollibus & Mattisyn Elizabeth

www.idlpublishing.com

DEDICATION

I dedicate this book to my Everything, King of Kings, Lord of Lords, The Lover of my soul. Without Him, this book wouldn't be written; not even in my best efforts could I finish a good book on my own, but all things are possible through Christ Jesus Who strengthens me. I love the mystery of The Holy Trinity, all of Them are the same God, They're all one, yet, They also play different parts. It's like ice, water, and water vapor… They're all the same, but they take different forms for different reasons! My work is dedicated to my Abba, my Jesus, and my Holy Spirit; I cannot and will not do anything apart from Them. He is entwined in all I do, He is entwined in all of me, He is my inspiration and motivation; He pours His creative honey into my soul, then creates through me. All glory and honor be to Him, He is The Artist, I am the vessel which He chooses to send His art through. A million words couldn't even carry the weight of His glory. Abba, Jesus, Holy Spirit, thank You, I love You the most forever.

"Nothing I do is from my own initiative. As I hear the judgment passed by my Father, I execute those judgments. And my judgments will be perfect, because I seek only to fulfill the desires of my Father Who sent me." - John 5:30 TPT

Mattisyn Elizabeth ♥

CONTENTS

Acknowledgments

Prologue 1

1 Lyrics 7

2 Prom? 13

3 The Dress 25

4 The Storm 35

5 Yellow Hearts 43

6 Tell Me About It 57

7 Donuts and Decisions 67

8 What Do I Do? 73

9 Bailiffs and Breakfast 81

10 Back to School 93

11 The Assembly, The Truth, The Switch 99

12 Assembly II 105

13 The Question 113

14 The Hideout 121

15 Flowers 131

16 Say "I Do" 135

17	Forever? Yes, Forever.	143
18	Conversations	153
19	Free Time	157
20	Secret Service	163
21	Prom, and Maybe More.	167
22	Parties, Packages, and Police	177
23	Recovery	191
24	Graduation	197
25	Everything Else	201
	About the Author	213

ACKNOWLEDGMENTS

I would like to thank my Tribe who rallies around me in support, love, endless laughter, and constantly points me back to Jesus.

I would like to thank my Triangle for always supporting me, loving me, teaching me, and being used by the Lord to raise me up in the way that I should go. You ladies are my best friends.

Auntie, thank you, I love you. Words could not express how grateful I am to have a forever best friend like you.

PROLOGUE

Have you ever watched a movie, or read a book, or even seen an IG post about two best friends; the kind that makes you fall in love completely with the idea of friendship? It always seems absolutely fairytale, right? Like, nothing ever goes wrong, and even if it does, you know that in a few pages, or at the end of the hour, or on the next couple posts, everything will be alright. Absolutely inseparable, making those besties part would crumble their worlds.

It sounds great, a kindred spirit to share all of your adventures with, I mean, who doesn't want that? Somebody who understands you, who can read your mind and finish your sentences; someone who knows exactly what you're saying because of one look, that is the ultimate friendship. Somebody who lifts you up, doesn't leave you down in the dumps, and instead of competing with you like a "pick-me-girl", actually cares to see you flourish. Some say it's unattainable, I say, it's Quinn.

Hi, I'm Brylee, weird name right.. or maybe unique? My dad's name is Bryan, and my mom's name is KaraLee; you can put two and two together. Anyways, that is not the story I'm telling, at least not right now, no, this story isn't about my parents, my past, or even just about me; this is the story of my unbreakable friendship.

For starters, it's never boring; we're both very eccentric.. that's how people say "weird" kindly. We're SO eccentric that a lot of people have told us to start our own reality show, they were probably joking; be that as it may, I've committed to journaling and hopefully getting those documentations published. When I say "journaling", I mean throwing all our adventures into my notes and figuring out how to organize them later.

Shall I give you a little bit of background on us? I shall. I suppose you want to know how old we are? We're both almost 18; Quinn is June 21st, and I'm July 5th, so yes, she is slightly older and never lets me forget it! We're graduating high school in 2 weeks, and senior prom is in a week and a half!! Quinn definitely acts like she's too cool for these, "basic teenage practices", (her words, not mine), but deep down, I know she wants to go; even if she shows up in a black dress and combat boots, which she probably will.

Sometimes, we seem like complete opposites, but, I happen to think that difference is one of the most important ingredients in the glue that holds a friendship together. If it was fun to be friends with a literal you, then there would —really— be no need for friends at all.

Moving on, we live in Friday Harbor, Washington! It's a fairly small town, but, it has these great little secluded spots, perfect for best friend hideouts. We have at least 5 different places that we like to think are solely ours; I just hope they go undiscovered for as long as possible, I've always pictured our kids becoming best friends and exploring them together, just like we did. I think it's equal parts sunny and rainy here, which happens to be the perfect environment for the mossy, wooded hideouts to live, (you gotta have balance, ya know?); plus, I love the sun, while Quinn loves the rain, so, it kinda just works out for us!

Quinn is an aspiring musician, she's a total one-woman-show; sis plays the guitar, ukulele, drums, piano, AND she sings! So talented, I know. One day she's gonna be all rich and famous, but for now, she's pretty excited about her local gigs in diners and bowling alleys, stuff like that; they pay her pretty well honestly, she makes $80 for a 45 minute show. Oh yeah, that reminds me! She NEVERRR spends her money either— (and TBH she's made it a part of her personality)— she's not famous yet but she's low-key ballin'; I won't expose her, but her savings account is in the tens of thousands for sure.

Another thing about my edgy bestie, she loves, and I mean LOVES to change her hair. Short, long, red, blonde, black and green split dye, wigs;

you name it, she's probably done it and isn't planning on giving her hair a break anytime soon. Currently, I'm pretty sure she's teetering on the edge of a rainbow roots situation; she is so unafraid and confident, seriously, if she ever showed signs of caring what someone thought of her, that'd be a shock to me.

She just lives wild and free, she can't be tamed; she is her, and she won't change herself even if her big personality makes you uncomfortable. That's something I truly admire about her, I'm not even sure she knows what having an insecurity feels like.

Quick background check on us, We've been best friends ever since the second grade; inseparable ever since, and Quinn basically lives with us 90% of the time because her parents travel so often, business purposes, they're doctors. We plan on attending the same college, that is if we choose to go.. knowing her parents, we'll be going. My parents want us to stay local, but we were looking at something like Berkeley; that's a ways a way though, no need to get into that right now.

I definitely have filled out my college applications like 10 times in the last week though; Quinn actually hid my computer from me because I wouldn't take a break, come to think of it, I need it back now, I'm gonna have to talk to her about that. Anyways, I think I've prepped you for what you're about to see, so, I'm just gonna get into it now. Keep up!

Chapter 1

LYRICS

It's four a.m., Quinn is sitting criss-cross-applesauce in the dark, guitar pick in mouth, humming and writing in her notes; the only trace of light is the brightness turned all the way up on her phone screen.

"Known each other since grade two, yeah me and you." **hums upbeat tune*.*

Brylee slowly wakes up, discombobulated, rolls over, and checks her phone to see that it's 4:10 a.m.

Groans "Q, what are you doing?".

Quinn, wearing her AirPods, continues writing, paying no attention to Brylee.

"Q.", *Brylee sits up, rubs her eyes and stares at her best friend until she comes into focus.* "Q.", *becoming frustrated, she throws a stuffed bear at her.* "Quinn!".

Taken by surprise, Quinn snaps around and rips out her AirPods.

"I'm so sorry! Did I wake you up?", she loudly whispered.

"Well there's no point to whisper now.", Brylee said, flopping back down in bed. "What are you doing anyways?".

"I was asleep, and then this melody danced right into my head and I didn't wanna forget it, so I jumped up and recorded myself humming it; and right when I was about to lay back down, suddenly, some lyrics joined the dance and a half completed song was doing a whole, like, flash-dance in my brain. You know me I—

"Couldn't let it escape you, I know.", *Brylee huffed as she pulled her blanket up over her face.* "We have school tomorrow, bruh, go back to bed.".

Quinn picked up her guitar and started softly strumming the tune that she'd been humming.

"I know, I'm coming right now.", *she said as she kept playing.* "I just need to see if there's anything else here.".

Brylee rolled her eyes, put her pillow over her ears and forced herself back to sleep. Not too long after the sun made its debut through their sheer, lavender curtains, Quinn's 5:30 alarm started blaring, waking up everyone, but her.

"Quinn!", *Brylee jumped out of bed and rushed to find the phone so she could snooze the alarm.* "Quinn! Princess Quinn!! Q! Where's your phone?! Ugh.", *she frantically searched for the incessant ringing and finally found it under Q's guitar.* "Gotcha!", *she grabbed the phone, silenced it, threw it on airplane mode, and put it on the charger at 12%; being the free spirit that she is, Quinn is SO bad about charging her phone.. it always ends badly too cuz her parents think she's ignoring them. I always have to let her use mine, so when I can, I just charge it for her.*

Brylee dragged herself into the bathroom and started getting ready; about 30 minutes later, she made her way back into the bedroom to find that Quinn was still knocked out.

"She's creative, I'll give her that, but sometimes that creativity costs her. She doesn't exactly balance it out, she's gung-ho about her projects and then she forgets to eat, or doesn't sleep.. or misses homework assignments. Most times, I find myself taking care of her, but, I really don't mind, that's what you do for family."

"Q, wake up.", *Brylee shakes her,* "Time for school, get up. You're gonna be late.".

Quinn twitched a little bit but remained deep asleep. She was hanging half way off the bed, drool falling from her open mouth like Amazonian rain on her pillowcase; one hand hanging on the floor and the other bent from the elbow, hovering above her messy hair, like that meme of Ana. The blanket was wrapped around her and the sheets were pulled from the edge of the mattress.

"Oy, you're such a rough sleeper.", *Brylee whispered to herself.*

She proceeded to grab Q an outfit, lay out her morning essentials, and brew some coffee.

"There's only 2 surefire ways to wake this girl up when she's that tired, fresh coffee, and sizzling bacon, so, coffee it is.".

As the coffee poured into the carafe the smell traveled through the halls into their bedroom. The scent of coffee beans was so thick that if they lived in a cartoon, you would've seen a wavy line in the air traveling swiftly to Quinn's nostrils until the blissful smell carried her off into the kitchen.

"Just as I knew it would happen, Quinn slowly walked into the kitchen, smiling and running her hand through her, somehow flawless, silky, black hair.".

"Goooodmorningg best frAnd! Beautiful day today! I just feel so alive! We're almost graduated adults, music is flyin' at me like a bee to a flower, and I live with my bestie!! Life is so good, what are we doin' today?", *Quinn hopped up on a barstool and adjusted her baggy hoodie that was falling off her shoulder.*

Brylee smirked, finished making Quinn her vanilla iced coffee, turned around, and set it in front of her.

"Very beautiful day, very EARLY day, but yes, beautiful.".

"Ooh coffee, thanks gurl!", *Quinn grabbed her glass with her hoodie sleeves covering her hands and brought the straw to her mouth.* "You know me, I love that.", *she said as she started sipping her drink.*

"I'm glad you feel that way, I want you to shut off your alarms.", *Brylee firmly demanded.*

"Wait, why? I need them to wake up!", *Quinn blurted, almost spitting out her coffee.*

"Like you said, I know you, and I know that everyday your alarm goes off so, SO early and you are un-phased; yet I am abruptly awakened by the sound of "Watermelon Sugar" playing at full volume. It doesn't stop there, Harry screams at me for an additional 10 minutes while I frantically search for your mostly dead phone, to silence him. Harry is a vibe, but I don't want

Lyrics   9

him yelling those vibes in my ear at the break of dawn.", *Brylee shot Q a look that said "you know I'm right", and took a sip of her coffee.*

"Okay fine, so what I'm hearing is, you'd like me to change the alarm sound??", *Quinn chuckled, teasing Bry.*

"I will eat all the bacon before you wake up for the rest of the year if you —

Quinn quickly cut her off.

"Whoa whoa whoa, okay, no alarms!", *Quinn took out her phone faced it toward Brylee, and cancelled all of her alarms.*

"Thank you.", *Brylee said with a smirk.*

"Okay well, aside from sleeping through alarms, be proud of me, I remembered to charge my phone! Look, 100%!!!", *Quinn slid her phone across the counter.*

Brylee picked up her phone and looked at the battery.

"Quinn, that was—, that was awesome, good job.", *Brylee congratulated her.* "She just looked so happy, what's the point of telling her I plugged it in? I mean, she just deleted all her alarms for me, there's no point to nitpick.". "Dude, you better go get ready, I'll heat us up some breakfast burritos.".

Quinn grabbed her phone and coffee, and gracefully slid off the barstool.

"You right, BRB.", *Quinn hopped up on the counter, high-fived Brylee, jumped down and ran off shouting,* "Teamwork makes the dream work!!!"".

Brylee laughed and thought to herself, "It really does take a village.". As the minutes passed, they came closer and closer to being late for school; with Brylee coordinating prom, she couldn't afford to be even thirty seconds late.

"Are you ready?!

Food is ready!", *Brylee shouted to Quinn,* "If we want to be on time you better be ready, dude.".

"Almost, just eat! I'll eat on the way!", *Quinn replied.*

As soon as Brylee sat down with her food, her phone started buzzing. It was a text from her family group-chat.

Mom: "Honey, we'll be home late tonight, I'm gonna send you girls some money for food.".

Dad: "We're gonna be home late?".

Mom: "We literally have that gala tonight, it runs till midnight.".

Bry: "Thanks, Mom.".

AppleCard Transfer: $250.00 to Brylee Hannah Brown's Checking Account ending in 9554 from KaraLee Francis Brown's Savings Account ending in 4253.

Dad: "Since when does pizza cost a small fortune?".

Bry: "Thanks, Mom, I love you. Love you too dad.".

Mom: "I want the girls to be set, we'll be gone for a while, they might wanna go do something. I love you too, Sweetheart! See you tomorrow.".

Dad: "Okay, love you, Bry-Bry.".

Brylee sets her phone down, and as she takes a bite, Quinn slides into the kitchen.

"According to my calculations, we've gotta go, kid! Aren't you ready?", *Quinn grabs her burrito and starts shoving it down as she slings her backpack over her shoulder, car keys dangling from her finger.*

Brylee looks at her the way you'd look at someone whom you've tried to get out the door for an hour.

"Your calculations are correct, lez go then!", *Brylee slammed her coffee, put the cup in the sink and shoved her burrito in her mouth as she grabbed her things.* "By the way, my parents are gonna be home late, so, girl's night?", *she asked with a full mouth, as they rushed out the door.*

"Betttt.", *Quinn dragged her response into a song and slammed the door behind them.* "I'm driving!", *Q held up the keys excitedly and jumped in the driver's seat.*

Brylee laughed, got in the car, and turned up the radio as Quinn pulled out of the driveway. She connected her phone, put on their song, and they sang along screaming out the words for every driver in Friday Harbor to hear.

Chapter 2

PROM?

As soon as we walk through the outer cafeteria doors to enter our school, we see promposals flooding the multipurpose room. Girls giddy with excitement because their crush is asking them out for the first time; boys nervously holding up homemade signs and performing to iconic songs, holding out hope that the prettiest girl in their world will accept their offer. While I find it slightly romantic, Quinn finds it incredibly dorky; or so she says.

"Ew.", *Quinn forced a gag.*

"C'mon, you're telling me if someone went through all the trouble of promposing to you, you'd just reject it without giving it a second thought?", *Brylee tried to reason,* "I think it's romantic in a way, someone putting themselves out there like that… I think I might say yes.".

"Cool, then I wouldn't have to go.", *Quinn smirked, knowing that Bry was about to go on her senior year rant.*

"We, as in me AND you, are going to prom. It is SENIOR prom, this is SENIOR year; this is supposed to be the best year of our school lives! We're supposed to gain all kinds of freedoms and do unforgettable things that we get to tell our kids about someday!!! I don't care what you say, you're going. In fact, we have food at home, we're using that money to prom shop after school.", *Brylee smiled, excited at the thought of trying on dresses with her best friend.*

"But—

"No buts! We're doing this, we each only have three classes left, we should be out by one.", *nothing could change her mind at this point.*

"Fine. No glitter though, that's my policy.", *Quinn grumbled.*

"I'm so excitedddd!!!", *Brylee squeaked.*

Quinn giggled and rolled her eyes at her best friend's enthusiasm, just then, the bell rang and the principal walked in.

"Okay ladies and gentlemen, ALL promposals must cease until after school. It's finals week, we need NO distractions. I repeat, NO distractions. Run to class, good luck on testing!", *Mrs. Shay announced through the P.E. teacher's bullhorn.*

Mrs. Shay smiled and waved Brylee over.

"What does she want?", *Quinn asked, a bit perplexed.*

"Oh, you know, prom stuff probably. I'll catch you after class!", *Brylee quickly hugged Quinn and sped over to the principal.*

Quinn headed to class and Brylee gave Mrs. Shay a big hug, they were kindred spirits in a way; both bubbly as ever, usually.

"Well, hello Ms. Brylee! How are the prom preparations coming along? Everything on theme and on schedule? You know there's only a few days left to secure the details.", *Mrs. Shay questioned her favorite student.*

"Yes, ma'am! On schedule, on theme, below budget, and as fabulous as ever if I do say so myself!", *Bry enthusiastically reported.*

"Great! I knew I chose the right girl for the job. Oh! Also, before I forget, I want to talk to you about something after class, do you have time to meet me in my office; or do you and Quinn have plans?".

"Oh, uhm… yeah, I can meet you, I finish all my classes around 12:50; Quinn and I are going prom shopping, so we were gonna meet up with each other after our last class, can she join?".

"I prefer to speak to you privately, Quinn can sit outside my office if you'd like.", *Mrs. Shay replied hesitantly.*

"Okay, no worries.", *Brylee nervously chuckled,* "Am I in some sort of trouble?", *she asked with a shaky tone.*

"Oh dear, no! Are you kidding me?! My star student in trouble 2 weeks before graduation? Never. It's good news! Be excited. You better hurry off to class now, try not to think about our meeting too much; you need to focus.", *shocked that Brylee would assume she was in trouble, the principal laughed her answer in a reassuring tone.*

"Oh good! I'll try not to, see you around one!", *Brylee slightly giggled in relief.* "Clearly she doesn't know me like I thought she did, I'm gonna be reflecting on this more than my test answers.", *she thought to herself.*

Mrs. Shay patted her on the back and sent her off to class. As she approached her classroom, she saw that they had already put up the "students testing" sign, and she knew the door was locked.

"Noo.. no, no, no, this can NOT be happening to me right nowww.", *she nervously whined. Embarrassed, she knew what she had to do.*

She slowly approached the door, cringing, and gently knocked 3 times. The door opened, letting out the most torturous creak, a cold gust of air, and that weird carrot smell that classrooms get. Behind the door was her teacher, Mr. Daily, and he did not look happy.

"Mr. Daily, I'm so sorry, I was——, *Brylee stammered.*

"I don't want to hear excuses Ms. Brown.", *He said sharply,* "I just want you to get to your seat and begin your exam.", *he stepped aside so she could enter.*

"Yes, Sir.", *Brylee replied, pulling her eyes away from his cold glare.*

As she cautiously tip-toed into the classroom, every single student perked up and stared at her; their eyes felt like lasers shooting red-hot beams of judgment straight at her. She directed her eyes at her feet, ignoring them, and settled at her desk. Just as she flipped to page 1 of 20 in her test booklet, a small, folded piece of notebook paper fell out. She glanced up at her teacher to find him reading at his desk; once she decided that no-one was paying attention to her, she carefully unfolded the note.

"Dear, Brylee,

I noticed that no-one has asked you to prom yet. I've been thinking about this moment all year and I wondered if I should orchestrate a flash mob, or write you a song, but, I figured that you were more of an old-school-letter-type-girl. I hope I made the WRITE decision, (Hah, see what I did there?). Anyways, if in fact you don't have a date, I would be TRULY honored if THEE Brylee would accompany me to the single most important event of our educational lives, (Did that even make sense? Educational lives?). Anyhow, this is a formal invitation , please circle an answer, Mi'lady.

Yes.   No.

Your's Truly,

Jason McKinley."

Brylee smiled wide and glanced behind her to see Jason nervously looking at her in expectancy, awaiting her answer. As excited as she was, she couldn't shake the feeling that she needed to go to her senior prom with her best friend. Her wheels were turning and an idea popped into her head, if someone asked Quinn to the prom, they could be double dates! "There were many guys at this school who liked Quinn, she just never paid any attention. If somebody went through the trouble of creating the perfect promposal for her, I know she couldn't turn it down.", Brylee looked back at the note, grabbed her pencil, and created a new category

"MAYBE."

She circled it, hid the note in her pocket, and began her exam. As the minutes ticked by, she came closer to finishing her exam, meanwhile, Quinn has already finished hers.

Hums and quietly sings, "Best friends since grade 2—

"Quinn, stop humming, that is unacceptable during exam hours, other students are trying to focus!", *Mrs. Delaney snapped at her.*

"But, what if I'm done? What do I do?", *Quinn challenged her teacher.*

"Then double check your work, we've gone over this.", *her teacher replied, annoyed at her retort.*

"I've triple checked.", *Quinn stared blankly at her teacher with a single eyebrow raised.*

"That's near impossible, we started 30 minutes ago. You're either cheating, or a genius… or you circled all C's and hoped for the best.", *her teacher condescendingly chuckled, as the class watched their back and forth.*

"Awe, it's so kind of you to call me a genius, I didn't know you felt that way, teach.", *Quinn replied, knowing she would get under the teacher's skin.*

"Fine. Then turn your test into me to grade, and since you're so sure of yourself, no retakes.", *the teacher threatened.*

"Cool.", *Quinn stood up, dropped her test off, threw up a peace sign and walked out while telling the class,* "Good luck.".

Mrs. Delaney got up and locked the door after she left.

"Anyone else wanna risk not being able to retake this?", *she rhetorically asked the class in a firm tone.*

The class quickly shifted their eyes to their papers and the only sound left was the scribble of pencils filling in test bubbles.

"That's what I like to see.", *she announced in a callously satisfied timbre.*

Meanwhile, Quinn has made her way down to Brylee's classroom, and had been sitting outside, against the wall for 5 minutes already, when she heard Mr. Daily announce that time was up. She hopped to her feet, gleefully awaiting her friend, but before Bry exited the room, Q felt a tap on her shoulder.

"Hey, Quinn.", *a deep, vaguely familiar voice caught her attention.*

Quinn turned around with a defensive look on her face.

"Hey, Reese, right?", *the words left her mouth quicker than she could think about her answer.*

"Yeah, I'm in Delaney's class with you; I just wanted to say I thought it was super cool, the way you stood up to her like that.", *Reese nervously complimented her.*

"Oh, thanks. Yeah, it was no biggie.".

Awkward silence filled the air for about 30 seconds, until they both tried to break it at the same time.

"So—, *they both stumbled over each other.*

"Oh! Sorry, you go first.", *Reese replied with a smile.*

"Thanks, no uhm, I was just gonna ask if that was all you came to tell me.", *Quinn countered, clueless that he obviously liked her.*

"Not exactly, I uh, I was just gonna ask…", *he stuttered, clearly shaken up about her.*

Quinn intensely stared at him, waiting for his next sentence.

"Could I maybe get your number? Schools out soon and I don't wanna lose touch, ya know.", *he tried playing it cool.*

"Oh, uh, I mean sure I guess, lemme see your phone.". *Quinn replied a bit confused as to why this guy wanted to keep in touch with her when they had never talked before.*

He handed her his phone, she quickly entered herself as a contact, threw up a peace sign, and took a selfie, for her contact photo. When she was finished, she handed him back his phone.

"That's me.".

"Bet, do you want me?", *Reese awkwardly asked.*

Quinn gave him a look that questioned their whole encounter.

"I mean… I didn't mean. Let me rephrase, do you want my number?", *he sheepishly tried to fix his mistake.*

"Bruh, just text me and I'll lock you in, Reese Spencer, right?", *Quinn nonchalantly brushed his awkwardness off.*

"Oh, right, cool, yeah that's my name.", *he assured her, surprised that she knew it.*

"Bet, that's a fire name by the way, I like it.", *she complimented him in the chillest tone you could imagine.*

Reese quickly made up an excuse to leave so he didn't make his intense nervousness any-more known to his crush.

"Thanks, Quinn. I'll text you later.", *he said while turning to walk away.*

"Cool, talk to you then.", *Quinn turned around to see that the classroom had cleared out, and that Brylee had watched that whole thing take place.*

"Oh my—

"Don't even do it.", *Quinn warned.*

"He likes you!", *Brylee squealed with the biggest smile painted across her face.*

"What? No, he doesn't.", *she tried shrugging that thought off.*

"I promise you, he does. Did you not notice the hearts in his eyes, or the nervous sweating??", *Brylee pleaded.*

"Gross.".

"Okay, yes, the sweat is kind of gross, but the rest is so cute!", *Brylee argued her point.*

"Okay, I'm done with this conversation. Speaking of conversations, what did Mrs. Shay want?", *Quinn curiously asked.*

"Oh no!", *Brylee shrieked.*

Watching Quinn and Reese, she completely lost track of time, it's now 1:15.

Prom? 19

"What's wrong?", *Quinn questioned, a bit concerned.*

"Can you go to the car? I'll be right out, I was supposed to meet her at one.".

Brylee rushed down the halls before Quinn could even respond, she was running so fast along the freshly waxed floors that she tripped and slid 3 classrooms down. Suddenly, Jason rushed to her side.

"BRYLEE! Are you okay?! Let me take you to the nurse's office!", *he knelt beside her, helping her up.*

"Great, what are the chances?", she thought to herself.", "No, I'm fine, really! Thank you.", *Brylee forced herself to her feet and swiftly began walking away.*

"Wait! You dropped something!!", *Jason shouted.*

Brylee turned the corner, ignoring him, and disappeared from his sight.

"Is that my note?", *he whispered to himself.*

He bent down, picked up the piece of paper and began unfolding it. He skipped all the way to the bottom and noticed that she added an extra option. "Maybe?", *he thought,* "Classic Bry.". *As he was folding it back up he noticed her number written on the back with a little smiley-face next to it; excited, he took out his phone, created a contact for her, and sent a message.*

+1-755-432-0809

"Be more careful next time, hall monitor might dirty up that squeaky clean record with a speeding violation. ;) :D."

Brylee felt the buzz but ignored it as she rushed into the principal's office. She started explaining herself before Mrs. Shay had a chance to get a word in.

"Mrs. Shay, I'm so so sorry, I totally lost track of time, Quinn had a moment and I got—

"Brylee, calm down, it's okay, we said around one, not exactly one.", *Mrs. Shay cordially chuckled,* "Go ahead and take a seat, this will only take a few moments.".

Brylee took a seat, crossed her legs, and looked up in wonder at her principal.

"As I've told you many times before, you are this school's star student. I wanted to give you this news personally, instead of in an email, although I'll send you home with a signed letter to confirm what we talk about.", *Mrs. Shay walked around her desk to Brylee and took a seat beside her,* "I've nominated you to be this year's valedictorian!!!", *she excitedly dropped the news.*

Brylee remained frozen in shock, jaw dropped, staring at Mrs. Shay.

"Brylee! Say something! Aren't you excited?! You ought to be so proud of yourself!", *Shay energetically explained.*

Brylee finally broke her starstruck gaze.

"Yes! Of course I'm excited, it's just a huge honor and it was so unexpected, I didn't even know that several people were nominated! I needed to process.", *Brylee chuckled, getting teary-eyed with an overwhelming sense of gratitude.*

"Aweeee, only two people are nominated; the vice principal nominated the other candidate, we're not allowed to know who each other chose though. I'm gonna miss you, promise to visit me here sometimes, even after you graduate!", *Mrs. Shay insisted, also becoming teary-eyed.*

"Of course I will Mrs. Shay, you have my number, text me anytime. After I graduate we're just friends, there's no student/teacher barrier. You can go out with Quinn and I to lunch sometime!", *Brylee compassionately assured her.*

"That's so sweet, you're a doll. I'll definitely take you up on that. Run along now, go have fun shopping; you and Quinn be safe.".

"Always.", *Brylee replied with a soft smile.*

The two of them hugged, and Brylee calmly walked out of her office, once she reached the hallway, she began running once again. Excitement flooded her body, and butterflies fluttered around her stomach at the thought of their soon to be best night ever.

She finally made her way outside and bolted to her car where Quinn was waiting. She had her music blasting so loud that you could hear it from inside the school; as Bry approached the car, she pulled out her phone and started recording her. Through the windshield you could see Q belting out the songs, and putting on a very animated show.

As Bry continued to record, she couldn't control her laughter, and she let out a screaming belly laugh; Quinn spotted her, then started putting on an even goofier performance. Brylee eventually stopped the video as it became shakier from her uncontrollable laughter, and she hopped in the passenger seat. As soon as she sat down, she plugged in her phone, and acted like nothing happened, knowing that Quinn would be desperate to hear about her meeting.

"Soo?", Quinn said expecting Brylee to spill about her meeting.

"So?", Brylee teasingly retorted.

"Fine, don't tell me.", Quinn shifted into drive, unbothered.

"Okay fine! You cracked me! You know I have to tell you. Put the car back in park.", Bry anxiously shouted.

Quinn parked the car and looked at Brylee.

"I'M A NOMINEE FOR VALEDICTORIAN!!!", she screamed with excitement.

Quinn dove over her seat and hugged Brylee so tightly, I'm surprised she didn't explode.

"I'M SO PROUD OF YOU!!! BRY THIS IS AMAZING, YOU'VE BEEN DREAMING ABOUT THIS SINCE THE 5th GRADE! We have to call your parents!", Quinn yelled, matching her bestie's energy.

Q charged at the car screen to press the phone app, but in all the excitement she selected the text app by mistake, and Jason's message played.

"Be more careful next time? Who was that? What happened?", *Quinn looked at Bry perplexed.*

Brylee looked down at her lap and chuckled, remembering the note and the accident.

"Earth to Brylee. Who was that? A boy perhaps?", *Quinn poked at her.*

"Perhaps.", *Brylee replied with a mysterious smile.*

"Gurl, who?!", *Quinn demanded.*

"Start driving, I'll tell you on the way.".

The girls buckled in, Quinn shifted into drive, and started toward the mall.

Chapter 3

THE DRESS

The girls pulled into the mall's parking structure just as Brylee had finished catching Quinn up on everything she missed.

"That was so much to take in, exciting, but a lot.".

Quinn found a space and parked.

"So Jason finally asked you out, huh? When?".

"I wouldn't really call it a date, I don't know. It's more of a hangout, and I was thinking you could come?", *Brylee suggested.*

Quinn broke out into a sarcastic laughter.

"Let me get this straight, this guy that you've liked since the 8th grade finally has the guts to ask you out… and you don't have the guts to actually go on the date?", *Q stared at Brylee knowing that what she said was true.*

"That's not it, I just—

"What? Feel bad leaving me at home? Don't. I'm not gonna third-wheel, besides, I have other friends.", *Quinn joked, turning up her nose as she exited the car.*

Just then, Brylee matched the sarcastic laughter that Quinn used before.

"No you don't, by 'friends' I think you mean projects. Unless of course…", *Brylee smirked in Q's direction,* "Unless you're referring to Reese.", *her smile grew wider, as she tested her friend.*

"Reese who?", *Quinn retorted, trying to block out the idea of a crush.*

"You know, that guy that makes you feel tingly all over when I mention him.".

"Please don't use the phrase, 'tingly all—

"The one that thinks you're 'cool', or whatever.".

"More like the, 'or whatever'", *Quinn mumbled.*

"The one that definitely wants to take you to—

"Don't even say—

"PROM!".

"Sigh.", Quinn shook her head, acting annoyed and disinterested.

As they walked into the mall, Brylee kept messing with Quinn, amused at the fact that her usually cool and collected best friend was totally flustered.

"Are you honestly telling me that if Reese made you a wholeee promposal, you would just say, 'nah', and walk away?", *Brylee practically interrogated Q.*

"What does it even matter?", *Quinn seemed embarrassed.*

"Why are you so embarrassed if you—

Quinn cut Brylee off just as they walked through the entrance of the dress shop.

"BECAUSE I'VE NEVER HAD A CRUSH ON AN ACTUAL, REAL LIFE PERSON BEFORE!", *Quinn shouted through gritted teeth.*

Brylee was taken aback for a moment, worried that she had taken the whole Reese thing too far; but the shock quickly wore off as she realized that Quinn had actually admitted to liking someone. As they stared at each other, an employee interrupted their 'colorful' conversation.

"Welcome in, girlies! Everything to the left side of the store is 60% off; and all the dresses that sweep the floor are buy one get one! Do you need help finding anything?", *she shouted at the girls with a perky tone.*

"No, we're fine, thanks!", *Brylee politely replied.*

"Okay! If you need me, my name is Val, I'll be happy to help!".

"Appreciate it, Val", *Quinn broke her silence.*

Val carried on fixing their prom display and adding new accessories to the mannequins while the girls started browsing.

"What size are you again? I know medium, but like, what number size?", *Brylee asked Quinn as she ruffled through a rack.*

"I don't know, somewhere between 4 and 10 I think… I wear medium/large, it just depends.", *Quinn followed Bry as she waltzed through the store like it was her home, like she owned the place.* "I'm sorry for making a scene, I just, I don't know, it's new.", *she softly apologized.*

"I forgive you, I'm sorry for prying. I just want you to be happy, whatever that looks like.", *Brylee pulled a dress and hung it on Quinn's shirt,* "Too short?", *she asked as she kept looking.*

"No, it's fine. Brylee, I—

"You look great in greens and blues! How about a mint look, I think you —

"Bry!", *Quinn exclaimed,* "Look at me, I don't care about color swatches right now. What do I do?! You're my best friend, you're supposed to help me with this stuff!!!".

The Dress

"Finally! Ugh, I've been waiting for you to ask for my help. Okay, so here's what we're gonna do,—

"We?", *Quinn asked.*

"Yes, we. If getting you out of bed is a team effort, so is this. We are in everything together.", *Brylee answered with a tone that screamed, "obviously".*

"True. Okay, continue.", *Quinn began looking at accessories as she listened to the plan.*

"Okay, so, we start with the dress. By the time he asks you to prom, which, mark my words, he will, all he has to worry about is matching his tie and the corsage.", *Brylee smiled, satisfied with her solution.*

"What about when he texts me?", *Quinn asks earnestly.*

"Wow, okay.. girl, I know you're my best friend, but you're gonna have to give me something to work with here. Now, when somebody texts you, you use your thumbs to press letters, which form sentences, then—

"BRYLEE!".

"Kidding, I'm just kidding!", *she snickered,* "We'll worry about that when it happens. Right now, just relax and have fun! We're shopping, there's no room for anxiety. Wow, who would've thought I'd ever be the one telling you to calm down?", *Brylee muttered.*

"You're right. You're right! It'll be fine, great even! So, back to you, who's the other nominee.. and did J ever text you back?", *she quizzed Bry.*

"I don't know, the VP picks the other one, and apparently, they can't tell each other who they chose. As for Jason, no, not yet, I don't really know how to respond; all I did was add him as a contact.", *she admitted.*

"Bruh, lemme see that, I'm about to handle this.".

Quinn swiftly grabbed Brylee's phone and began composing a text message.

To: Jason M.

"I know right, so, nansjsnaklakwekememememmememensmsmsmkLkkjjaksk—

Brylee dropped the dresses, tackled Quinn, and tore her phone out of her hands.

"Dude, are you insane?!", *Quinn hollered in a hush tone and began picking up the clothing.*

"How are you gonna have a breakdown because you don't know what to do about Reese, but then suddenly, you know exactly what to say to Jason?!", *Bry finished deleting the message.*

"Easy, because Jason isn't my problem. I'm on the outside of that, B, so it's easy to look in and quickly locate the best decision. That's why you don't know what to say to him, but you apparently know how to help me with my thing.", *Quinn explained while staring at her friend.*

Brylee rolled her eyes and handed Quinn her phone, admitting that she was absolutely right. She then noticed Q putting a dress back on the rack.

"What are you doing?! What did you put back?", *Brylee exclaimed.*

"I said, no glitter.", *Quinn shot Brylee a dry look and began recreating her message to Jason.*

To: Jason M.

"I know right, so anyways, when do you want to go out?"

...

Jason M.

"What do you mean? LoL, on prom."

Quinn looked up at Brylee confused.

"Bry, I thought you didn't know when he wanted to take you out.", *Quinn questioned.*

"That's what I said.".

Quinn showed Brylee the conversation.

"It looks pretty clear to me.".

"HE ALREADY RESPONDED?!", *Brylee hollered.*

"Did he or did he not ask you to prom?".

"He did.", *Brylee shyly responded.*

"And, did you or did you not say yes?".

"I said, 'maybe'".

"Why?!?! Do you know how long you've been waiting for this?!".

"I know…".

"Hold up, don't tell me it's because of me.", *Quinn locked eyes with Bry.*

Brylee ignored her and kept grabbing dresses.

"Brylee Hannah Brown. Is that why?".

"Maybe..".

"NOO. What were you thinking??? I'm not gonna miss prom if I don't go, but if YOU don't go with Jason, you're gonna regret it; and I refuse to be the reason you have regrets about, 'the greatest night of our academic lives'", *Quinn explained.*

"Academic lives, not educational, that's what he meant to say.", Brylee thought to herself.

"Hello?! Earth to Brylee!!".

"Yes, I heard you. I know. You're right! But, I still want you to come.".

"Dude, no. I don't have a date, and I wont be a third wheel. I'll stay at home and write.".

"You HAVE to come.", *Brylee implored,* "Are you telling me that if you have a date, you'll come?!", *she asked excitedly.*

"Maybe, IF that happens naturally, I don't want you orchestrating something and convincing some poor, unsuspecting guy to perform it. Got it?", *Quinn made herself very clear.*

"Got it. Now, let's find you the perfect fit!".

After about 3 hours the girls finally made their decisions, they in fact found the perfect dresses. They complimented one another, and fit each other's personalities perfectly. Brylee's comes mid thigh and is made of silk; honestly, it looks like a 1960's red carpet dream. It's baby pink with hot pink and orange, groovy squiggles; and of course, it's chalk FULL of glitter. She went with diamond studded, stiletto pumps, and a hot pink clutch to match.

Quinn on the other hand landed on a somewhat electric mint number; it sweeps the floor and has rhinestone straps. Technically, rhinestones aren't glitter. She completed her look with a rhinestone studded mini backpack purse, and 4 inch black combat-boots.

They were ecstatic with their purchases and felt that their planning process was complete. As they made their way back to the car, Quinn's phone started ringing.

Incoming Call From - Reese Spencer

    ACCEPT   *DECLINE*

"BRY.", *Quinn nervously shouted.*

"QUINN.", *Brylee replied, making fun of her.*

"He's calling me. What do I do?!", *she asked in panic.*

"Who? OH! Answer it!!", *Brylee insisted.*

Quinn hesitantly answered the phone, and all signs of nervousness went out the window. She sounded as if she had all the answers and definitely didn't have a minor panic-attack 5 seconds earlier.

"Hey, Reese, what's up?".

"Oh, hey, I thought I was gonna catch your voicemail to be honest.".

"I mean, if you want, you can hang up and call back, and I'll let it go to voicemail for you.", *Quinn replied with a snarky tone.*

"Teasing him already, wow, she must really be crushin'.", Brylee thought to herself.

"No, no! That's not what I meant, I meant—, *Reese began frantically explaining himself.*

"Dude, chill, I was just messin' with you. For real though, what's up?", *Quinn replied as cool as possible.*

"Oh, hah hah, yeah uhm, I was just wondering if you're busy tonight?", *he was clearly nervous as he asked.*

"I actually am busy tonight.".

"Oh, no worr—

Brylee shot her a look that read, "you better not turn this down.".

"I'm free tomorrow though.".

Reese felt a thousand butterflies zoom into his stomach.

"Great! Can I pick you up at three?", *he asked.*

Quinn looked at Brylee, expecting her to help her with the answer; Bry frantically nodded, and mouthed, "yes!".

"Yeah, bet, sounds good.".

"Cool, I'll see you tomorrow, Quinn.", *Reese exhaled in relief.*

"See you tomorrow, Reese, bye.".

Quinn hung up the phone, and they got in the car. As soon as she sat down, she let out a breath of relief.

"Dude, low-key, I'm nauseous.".

"You need me to drive?", *Brylee laughed.*

"Nah, I'm good.".

"You okay?".

Quinn turned and looked at her friend.

"Did I just agree to a date?", *she asked, looking for reassurance.*

"Yes, ma'am, you did.", *Brylee gave a joyful sigh,* "My Quinny is finally growing up.", *she teased while batting her eyes.*

"Shut uppp.", *Quinn chuckled as she pulled out of their parking spot.*

"For real though, I need food. Stop by Canes or something. Celebratory chicken tendies!!!", *Brylee shouted.*

The girls laughed and drove off.

Chapter 4

THE STORM

   Soon after Brylee's parents made it home last night, the biggest thunderstorm Friday Harbor has ever seen hit. It was terrible, we couldn't get any sleep; you might think that a thunderstorm would lull you right to bed, I mean, that's why people pay monthly for those apps right? Wrong! The only sound we heard all night were crashing trees and car alarms. However, we made the best of it, we modeled our prom fits for my mom, my dad of course had no problem staying passed out during the noise; so we pretty much had a girl's night with her.

   We watched movies with her all night, painted our toes, and literally braided each other's hair until we finally fell asleep all cuddled up around five o'clock in the morning. It's about nine now and we're all just getting up; dad is outside examining the damages, seeing if the neighbors need help.

   Thankfully, even though the tree in our backyard went down, it didn't hit anything. No shattered windows, no dented cars, zero damage. The wifi is finally back on, and what do you know, Quinn and I have several messages, and for once, they're not from each other.

   14 text messages from, Mom & Dad, and Reese Spencer...

"Bry!", Quinn whispered.

"Yeah?", Brylee replied.

"Did Jason text you?".

"Yeah, like 3 times, why?".

"Cuz, Reese texted me like 10 times, what do I do?".

"Well what did he say?".

"I don't know, I just saw his name and told you!", *Quinn exclaimed.*

"I'm gonna go out on a limb here and say a good start would probably be to read what he said.", *Brylee looked at Q and smirked.*

"Yeah, you're totally right, I don't know what I was thinking.", *Quinn tried playing it cool.*

Quinn opened up her phone and started reading through her notifications.

Reese Spencer

"Hey, Quinn."   9:45 p.m.

"It's gettin' pretty stormy out there, how is it for you?" 10:00 p.m.

"I'm excited about tomorrow!"   10:15 p.m.

"Wyd?"   10:39 p.m.

"Goodnight!"   11:15 p.m.

"Woah, trees are starting to crash, you okay over at your house?" 1:55 a.m.

"Quinn, you good??"   3:25 a.m.

"Idk if your wifi went out too but, text me when you can so I know you're okay." 4:01 a.m.

"Good morning!"   7:30 a.m.

"Quinn, fr, are you okay?"   *9:17 a.m.*

Quinn threw her head back and sighed to herself, assuming that Reese was no longer interested in her, considering she'd ignored him for close to 12 hours.

"Dude, what's wrong?", *Brylee asked in a concerned tone.*

"My first.. guy.. type thing and I already blew it.".

"How'd you blow it?", *Brylee questioned in confusion.*

"I ignored him and now he isn't interested anymore.", *Quinn grumbled as she threw her phone down.*

"He actually said that?", *Brylee asked as she picked up Quinn's phone,* "And, why were you ignoring him, low-key that's super rude.".

"He didn't say it, but I'm sure that's what he's thinking; and I didn't mean to, all his texts rolled in last night and this morning while everything was happening. I never got a chance to look at my phone, and after the wifi went out I figured, "what's the point?".", *Q laid back on the couch and put her arm over her face.*

Brylee opened up Q's phone and began scanning through their one-sided conversation.

"You are the dumbest smart person I know.", *Bry said in a monotone voice while shaking her head.*

"Way to make me feel better.", *Quinn shot a pitiful look at her.*

"HE LIKES YOU SO MUCH. How can you not tell?!", *Brylee threw the phone back at Quinn,* "HE'S WORRIED ABOUT YOU, text him back, NOW!", *she impatiently scolded.*

As soon as those words left Brylee's lips, Quinn sat up and a smile grew on her face.

"Wait, really?", *Quinn asked through her grin.*

"Hm, let me think, I don't know, YES.", *she answered as if it was SO obvious.*

"Okay, okay! I think I know what to say.", *she began typing out her message.*

To: Reese Spencer

"Reese! I'm so sorry, I'm great, thank you for checking in on me. Are you okay?! How's everything at your house? I'm excited for today too, I didn't mean to ignore you for nearly 12 hours, I just literally wasn't looking at my phone at all."
9:45 a.m.

Almost as soon as she sent the message, she received his reply; in complete and utter shock of how quickly he texted back, she started reading.

Reese Spencer

"It's okay, I'm just glad you're safe. I'm good, thanks for asking, a few trees crashed around us, but none did damage. A tree fell on my neighbor's car so I've been helping them clean that up. Are we still on for three? No worries, LoL, you might wanna start checking it more often, also, I'm sorry if I came on too strong. Ten messages may have been a little much, but, I wanted to make sure you were good."
9:45 a.m.

Quinn soaked up every last word he sent, then fell back on the couch with hearts in her eyes, and butterflies in her stomach. She'd never been interested in anyone before, let alone have them like her back. She'd never really been pursued, but she was starting to see the appeal.

To: Reese Spencer

"I guess I'm gonna have to get better about checking and charging my phone now that we're talking huh? LoL."   9:46 a.m.

"For me? Awe. I didn't think THE Quinn would make an adjustment like that for a newb, haha."

9:46 a.m.

"'Newb'? LoL, what a dork. Newb at what? Also, you didn't come on too strong, that was sweet, the way you checked up on me. I liked it."

9:47 a.m.

38   Prom in the Rain

"Newb in your life, ig. Also, cool, that's a relief. You're surprising me, Quinn, you're not exactly who I thought you were." 9:48 a.m.

"What's that supposed to mean? What did you think I'd be like?"
9:48 a.m.

"Hmm.. distant?" 9:48 a.m.

"Ouch." 9:48 a.m.

"I was taught, honesty is the best policy."

9:49 a.m.

"Honestly, that's refreshing. I appreciate that."

9:49 a.m.

"Something told me you would." 9:49 a.m.

"So, are we still on for 3?" 9:49 a.m.

"I believe we are.. Newb." 9:50 a.m.

"Sigh, you're not gonna let that go now, are you?"
9:50 a.m.

"Ahahahah!! That was cute. No, in fact, it's your contact name now. You had to know that was coming." 9:50 a.m.

   Attachment Type: Screenshot

"I kinda dig it. Yours is Q-tip." 9:51 a.m.

"LoL, no it's not." 9:51 a.m.

"Wanna bet?????" 9:51 a.m.

Attachment Type: Screenshot

"WHY?! Change it."   9:52 a.m.

"Haha, not a chance."   9:52 a.m.

"Whatever, I should just go back to ignoring you, bruh."
9:52 a.m.

"But, you won't. *Wink* See you at 3!"

                                  9:53 a.m.

Quinn began thinking to herself, "He's totally right, I'm not gonna ignore him. How did he just call me out like that? Is this what flirting feels like? Did I do it right!? I must've since he didn't get offended. Is this why girls in relationships think so much more? He is much more confident now than when we first talked. Oyyyy, I can't believe this is happening. Pull yourself together, Quinn!!". She proceeded to slap herself in a desperate attempt to snap out of her romantic haze.

"What are you doing, you weirdo?!", Brylee exclaimed as she watched Quinn smack her cheek.

"Waking up.", Quinn mumbled.

"We've been awake for like an hour now.", Bry replied almost as if she was asking a question.

"No, not like that.. and, an hour already?".

"Then like what? And, yeah, I've been texting Jason for the past 45 minutes.".

Quinn handed Brylee her phone and motioned for her to read the thread.

"I see I'm not the only one whose been busy texting.", she teased Quinn as she smirked. "Q, this is great, he's totally into you!".

"He waltzed right in like he had a wrecking ball set to tear down EVERY wall I have. Time to rebuild.", she replied.

"Eh, no. You're not rebuilding anything. That's what happens when you trust someone. Clearly your body is telling you that you can trust him, so embrace it, and don't be crazy.".

"But—

"Nope. No buts. Quit closing yourself off to everyone, otherwise, you're gonna end up an old plant-lady, asking to play your guitar at my house while I'm trying to spend time with my husband. You're always welcome, but, I refuse to see you turn into some wack, lonely 80 year old.".

"That escalated quickly.".

"Yes, things do.".

"Do you always live 100 years ahead in your brain?"

"Depends on the day. Now text him back.".

Quinn took a deep breath, braced herself, and began texting.

To: Newb

"See you soon."   11:00 a.m.

…

"*Blue heart emoji*"   11:01 a.m.

"Bry. What does the blue heart emoji mean?", *Quinn nervously asked.*

"It means soon you'll be replying with a red one.", *Brylee replied as she giggled,* "Just reply with a yellow one.".

"Are you sure?".

Brylee snatched Quinn's phone and sent the emoji.

"Done. Now, go get ready.", *she handed Quinn back her phone.*

Quinn looked at her in shock for a moment before she snapped out of it and dashed out of the living room.

Chapter 5

YELLOW HEARTS

Quinn was in the middle of ripping her closet apart in a desperate attempt to find the perfect outfit for her date, when Brylee walked in with a look of horror on her face.

"What?!", *Quinn exclaimed,* "You look more pale than usual, Bry, tell Jason to get you some sun.".

"No, yeah, I'm fine; I just didn't realize that we lived in an episode of Hoarders Extreme.", *Brylee calmly retorted in a sarcastic tone.*

"Really, 'Hoarders Extreme'? That was your reference of choice? I feel like you dialed in at 50% when you should've gone to 100, I mean there's more accurate and updated references, like—

"Quinn!", *Brylee interrupted in frustration.*

"Bry, don't be dramatic, I don't have that much stuff.".

"Maybe not, but, when you throw it all around our room like that, creating the 8th wonder of the world, 'Fashion Mountain', it looks like we need HGTV to come in and give our house a makeover.".

"Okay, this time you dialed in at like 65%, but, for real, what's up with these old—

"Quinn.".

"Okay, okay, we'll go with your HGTV thing. I would firstly like to say, I love that you find my fashion sense so epic that it not only qualified to be the 8th wonder of the world, but actually made it through. Secondly, that's honestly not a bad idea, we could use some new paint, or—

"Just make sure you clean up before you leave.", *Brylee softly demanded,* "Do you need some help? Do you want to borrow something?".

"Maybe if you just pick my clothes out for me, like before school, this will be less stressful. You know what I look good in, I'm your mannequin, go!", *Quinn announced like it was some sort of project runway challenge. Clearly this wasn't the first time they've used the, "I'm your mannequin" challenge as a solution to a fashion block.*

Quinn set a 60 second timer, and Brylee dashed into their closet to put together the perfect fit. She talked as she searched, as if somebody had a camera on her.

"You know, fashion really isn't that hard, it's like a puzzle. It's a little hard at first, but once you identify the corner pieces, and separate them from the middles, the whole thing starts coming into focus. Sometimes, you just have to start with a middle piece, and fit all the edge pieces around it. In other words, you can find a great accent piece, and identify what neutrals you need to make it a fit.", *Brylee rambled on.*

"15 seconds left on the clock, will Ms. Brown find this fit?! I think she will!! 14…13…12…11…10.", *Quinn counted down in a sport's announcer's timbre.*

"Ten seconds on the clock, I just need to find the matching shoe!", *Brylee squeaked,* "Ughh, Quinn it's such a mess in here!!".

"Clearlyyy that's a part of the challengeeee!!", *Q deepened her voice and dragged out her words.*

"I don't have enough time to look at you right now, but if I did, I would—

"5…4…….3…….2—

"Found it!!! Done! I'm done!", *Brylee shouted gleefully.*

"Congratulations! It is now time for you to DRESS YOUR MANNEQUIN!".

Brylee ran out of the closet and threw the pieces onto her bed.

"Oooooooo, so close! I see pink! You know what that means… DISSSSSQUALIFIED!", *Quinn hollered, still using her announcer's tone,* "Better luck next time, kid.".

"Very. Funny. However, the rules didn't clearly state 'No pink', therefore, I'm in and it's TIME TO DRESS MY MANNEQUIN!", *Brylee tried matching Q's tone.*

"It doesn't work for you, sorry.", *Quinn reverted to her normal voice.*

Brylee smiled and rolled her eyes in response.

"Whatever, just try this stuff on.", *Brylee ordered.*

Quinn forced a dramatically annoyed expression onto her face, her mouth hung open, her eyes stayed rolled back, and her head followed the lead of her eyes, permanently hanging back, making her emotions known. Despite her hesitancy, she walked over to the bed and began swapping out her clothes. The second she started changing, Brylee momentarily left to make their usual coffee orders.

"She's so stubborn sometimes.", *Brylee thought to herself as their coffee brewed. Suddenly, she was startled at the sound of Quinn's blood-curdling shriek.*

Bry bolted into their room as fast as she could, and rammed through the door.

"Quinn! What's wrong?! Are you okay!!!?", *she frantically asked.*

"I like it.", *Quinn replied in the most shocked tone.*

"What?".

"I actually like it. I didn't want to admit it, but I actually like my outfit. This might just be the best I've ever looked.", *Quinn admitted sheepishly.*

"I KNEW YOU WOULD!", *Brylee shouted confidently,* "Turn around, let me see it all.".

As Quinn twirled around, the full effect of her outfit couldn't be missed. She was wearing a sparkly, baby-pink, spaghetti-strap bodysuit; her high-waisted, wide-leg, baggy jeans were a distressed black, with tears strategically placed up and down her legs.

Her Vans were checkered and, black, with baby-pink laces, which pulled it all together. For jewelry, she had on a triple layer, stackable, gold necklace set, complete with her initial hanging just above the highest seam of her shirt; she had a ring on every other finger, and medium, thick, gold hoops to match.

Her hair was parted in the middle and pulled up into a half up half down pigtail look, which happened to be her favorite hairstyle; and put her blue streak on display. She looked breathtaking, Bry stood staring in awe of her friend's beauty, and of her own handiwork.

"Ahhhhh!", *Brylee squeaked,* "Gurll, you look so gooood!".

"He's gonna see me in glitter! Glitter, B, GLITTER!", *Quinn sat down on the bed, almost ashamed that she liked her clothes.*

"What does that matter if you think you look the best you ever have?", *Brylee asked, confused.*

"What if he doesn't like glitter? I never wear glitter, what if he thinks this isn't me or something?", *Quinn sighed with concern.*

"Was this it? Is this what it looks like when Quinn Darcy cares what somebody else thinks of her???", Brylee thought to herself before answering her best friend. "Quinn! Snap out of it! Stop worrying, if he doesn't like you because you're wearing a minimal amount of glitter, then he has no business taking up ANY of your time. Besides, I highly doubt any of that is gonna happen; also, he doesn't know you well enough to say, 'That's not you.', he's only seen you in the classroom. Now, go show him that after-school Quinn is just as confident as during-school Quinn!!! He's attracted to your confidence, not the fact that you mostly wear black.".

"You're right,. Thank you! You always know just what to say. How do you stay so calm about Jason?".

"Oh, girl, I'm just waiting for your crisis to be done before I drop the Jason one on you.", *Bry laughed.*

"Don't wait! I can handle both!", *Quinn reassured her friend that she's always there for her no matter what is going on in her life.*

"Okay, okay. He keeps pressuring me to give him an answer about prom. He's being really pushy to be honest, I just didn't think he was like that, and I'm a little concerned that if I keep asking for more time to think, he's gonna snap and take someone else.".

As Quinn heard those words leave Brylee's mouth, a fury burned within her at the thought of her best friend being pushed around.

"Look, Bry, I hate to say this, but, if he's pressuring you this much just to go to prom, and making you feel like you're doing something wrong by saying no; then what else is he gonna try to pressure you into at prom? I know you've liked him for a long time, but, he sounds kind of unstable, to be honest.", *Quinn cautioned her.*

"*Sigh.* Maybe you're right. I guess I don't have a prom date then.".

"SIS DON'T BE CRAZY! You have me! I may not be Jason, but, that just means you'll have more fun.", *Quinn smirked at Bry, in an attempt to make her feel better.*

"But, you're going with—

"Nope. Don't even go there, he hasn't even asked me yet. Even if he did, I'd still choose you.".

"*Sigh.* Okay, I'll tell him no.".

Brylee pulled out her phone and started texting Jason.

To: Jason M.

"Hey, um, I'm sorry, but, I'm not gonna be able to go to prom with you."

...

"Why? Because of Quinn? You told me 'maybe'! Does that mean nothing?"

Brylee started getting nervous as his tone was—clearly— getting heated; Quinn was shaking her head while reading over her best friend's shoulder.

"No, not because of Quinn."

"Then why? If you can't give me a reason, then I'm still showing up as your date next week."

Quinn was taken aback by his arrogance and altogether creepy energy. She was so infuriated at the way he was forcing himself into her friend's life, that, looking at her, you could almost see steam blowing from her ears.

"You're too pushy, that's the bottom line. It's unsettling, and I don't trust you like I thought I did. I guess having a crush from afar is different from getting to know the real person up close. It's the difference between the idea of you, and you. Based off of our conversation over the past few hours, I can tell that you're not someone who I want in my life. I don't mean to be harsh, I just want to draw a clear line in the sand."

...

"Wow. Gaslighting are we?"

"Wait, excuse me? How does that make sense? What did I do to gaslight you?"

"For starters, you lead me on ALL year, then, when I finally ask you out, you toy with me instead of giving me a direct answer. Lastly, you go making up all kinds of false accusations as an excuse, because you're too much of a coward to admit that you just wanna go with Quinn."

"Uhm, I haven't talked to you at all this year, in fact I've barely even looked your way since the 10th grade. I know that because Quinn always told me to go for it, but I was too shy too…"

"Whatever."

"Also, I didn't mean to, 'toy with you', I truly just needed a little time to think. I didn't know what I wanted to do, because all my life I've dreamed of going to prom with my best friend, but she has her own date, so if you wouldn't have been so pushy, I would've said yes."

"It's your loss anyways. A million other girls want to go with me. My locker is flooded with notes."

"Good! That makes me feel better, I'm glad that there's girls who want to go with you; I'm just not one of them. Oh, and lastly, these aren't 'false accusations', I have screenshots and I'll be sure to post them to IG and the school website so those girls can make sure you're really who they want to go with. I'm sure you don't mind, if this is truly gaslighting, then, you'll have even more girls who want to go to prom with you, purely because they'll feel bad for you."

. . .

. . .

Quinn and Bry started laughing at the fact that Jason didn't know what to say, but suddenly, they heard a whoosh of a message sending and the ding of it failing. They looked down and realized that she accidentally recorded a voice note of their laughs.

| | | |///| | | |-\\\\/// | | | | | |

Message unable to send. This wireless user has blocked your number. Contact +18009007800 if this is an error.

The girls once again looked up at each other and their laughter picked up.

"Gorlll! I didn't realize you was a lawyer.", *Quinn hyped Brylee up.*

Bry fell back on her bed in relief and deleted their text thread.

"What would I do without you?", *Bry rhetorically asked with an endearing look on her face.*

"Eh, probably the same thing I'd do without you.".

"And what's that?".

"Take a bus to Mexico and book some better gigs!", *Quinn teased.*

Brylee chuckled, rolled her eyes, threw a pillow at Q, and quickly sat up.

"What time is it?!", *Brylee frantically asked.*

"Uhhh… it's.. ONE!! When did that happen?!?!", *Quinn exclaimed.*

"Well I mean, between you tearing apart the room, the mannequin thing, all this freaking out and texting. Sounds about right.", *She calmly responded,* "You better hurry up and do your makeup though.".

"I haven't even had coffee yet! That is so unlike me!".

"Oh, thanks for reminding me!", *Brylee replied in a perky timbre and shuffled out of their room.*

"Dude! Where are you going?".

"Just start your makeup!", *Brylee shouted from the hall.*

About 10 minutes later, Brylee walked back into their room sipping her half drank iced coffee, holding a plate of bacon, some avocado toast, and Quinn's usual.

"Lifesaver! You brought me coffee AND bacon!! You really do love me!", *Quinn jumped up from the floor where she was sitting, doing her makeup, in front of the full-body mirror, and snatched her treats.*

"That was wild.", *Bry started laughing,* "I've never seen you move so fast in my life.".

Quinn squinted at her friend.

"WHAT IF I DON'T HAVE TIME TO POOP?!", *Quinn hollered, and just as she did, Brylee's dad walked through the open door.*

"Quinn, after all this time, I thought you knew the bathroom was just around the corner, complete with air freshener and everything. I know I won't judge you.", *imagine the most, "dad tone", you could think of, that's exactly how he said it.*

"Mr. Brown! I have a date!".

"With who?! I need to meet this young man. No one takes my Quinny out without talking to me first!".

"Dad.".

"It's settled, I'm gonna set him straight first. When's he coming?".

"At three, Mr. B. Three!", *Quinn exclaimed.*

"It's 1:20! I have to do my hair!", *Bryan ran out of the room, slammed the door behind him and yelled from down the hall,* "Babe! Where's my good comb?!".

Brylee giggled and looked at Quinn, she was still visibly nervous.

"I don't think your glitter is gonna be the thing that scares Reese off.", *Brylee teased as she nodded her head in the direction of her dad.*

"On the real though, bathroom?", *Quinn asked in a more serious tone.*

"Take your coffee and go. Go nowww.", *Brylee insisted.*

Quinn nodded in agreement, grabbed her coffee, and ran to the bathroom. While Brylee was waiting for her, she saw a text come through on Q's phone.

From: Newb

"Newb? Who's Newb?", she thought to herself, "Q!", *she shouted.*

"Yeah?", *Quinn replied through the bathroom door.*

"You got a text from 'Newb'?", *she informed her like it was a question.*

"IT'S REESE! Open it! What did he say?!".

Brylee opened their text thread.

Newb:

"Hey, Q-tip, I know we said 3, but, I'm already in your area. Any chance I can pick you up earlier?"

Brylee's eyes widened.

"HE WANTS TO GET YOU NOW!!", *she hollered.*

"BUT I HAVEN'T POOPED YET!!!". *Quinn screamed in concern.*

Just then, Brylee heard her parents snickering and talking.

"*Sigh*. Ohh, Bryan, we know entirely too much about these girls.", *KaraLee chuckled.*

"I find it endearing that they're so comfortable. How do I look?", *he asked.*

"Ready for prom.", *she responded sarcastically.*

Bry redirected her focus to her friend.

"Q!".

"Yeah?".

"If you can hurry up in there, I think my dad can distract him until you're done!".

"Bettt! Get my phone! Text him back, tell him, 'Bet, come get me.'!".

"Okay, okay! I'm doing it right now!", *Brylee composed the text,* "IT'S SENT!", *she shouted.*

"Mr. B!", *Quinn yelled.*

"QUINN!", *he matched her tone.*

"I NEED YOU TO TALK TO REESE UNTIL I'M OUT OF THE BATHROOM, PLEASEEEE!".

"BETTT!", *he replied, mocking her.*

"YOU'RE THE BEST!".

Shortly after he agreed, we heard a strong knock at the door.

"Gasp! It's him!", *Brylee aggressively whispered to her dad,* "I'll get it!!", *she raced to the door and opened it.*

Standing there was Reese in black skinny-jeans, old-skool Vans, and a band tee, clearly surprised that he caught Bry instead of Quinn.

"Hey, Bry, is Quinn here?", *he nervously asked.*

"Indeed! She lives here!—

"But, you've gotta talk to me before you can take her out, young man.", *Bryan cut in with a booming tone.*

"Hello, sir!", *Reese confidently replied,* "You must be Quinn's dad.", *he extended his hand for a handshake.*

"Kinda!", *Bryan answered in a peppy tone.*

While Bryan and Reese were talking, Brylee slipped away to find Quinn. She made her way to the bathroom, but the door was open. She headed towards their bedroom where Quinn was sitting in the corner, strumming her guitar and writing.

"Quinn! He's here! What are you doing?!", *Brylee exclaimed.*

"Working on my song.", *Q nonchalantly replied.*

"You need to be working on your soon to be relationship!".

"I can't go.".

"Oh we are NOT doing this again!", *Bry walked over to Quinn, snatched her guitar, put it on their bed, and pulled her up.*

"What are you doing?!", *Quinn hollered.*

"Saving you from regret.", *Bry took her hand and yanked her into the living room where Reese was.*

Quinn's stomach turned and tightened more and more the faster they walked.

"I can't believe you're—

"Hey, Quinn!", *Reese enthusiastically greeted her, and jumped up from his seat.*

"Hi.".

Bryan got up from his seat, and announced that he was leaving. As he walked by Quinn, he whispered.

"This is a good one! Have fun!".

Quinn smiled and squeezed Brylee's hand.

"I didn't know that you and Brylee lived together.", *Reese started up the conversation.*

"Y-yeah, we can get into that later. What time do you think we'll be back?", *Quinn asked with a slight nervous tone.*

"Well, Mr. Brown said to have you home by ten.".

"Well, Ms. Brown, says, have her home at nine. That's six and a half hours.", *Brylee cut in.*

"Bry!", *Quinn exclaimed.*

"No, no. It's okay.", *Reese chuckled,* "Something tells me I should listen to the best friend.".

Brylee smirked and motioned for them to leave.

"Alright, lovebirds, get out of here!", *Bry insisted.*

They began walking through the door.

"Love you, B! I'll text you when I'm on my way home.", *Quinn assured her.*

"Okay! Have fun! Be safe!".

As Reese walked by, Brylee stopped him.

"Aye, you don't want to know what happens if you hurt her.", *Brylee threatened the way any best friend would.*

"I promise, I won't.", *Reese patiently replied.*

He left, Bry shut the door and leaned up against it, relieved that Quinn decided to go, but nervous that her best friend was on her first date. Meanwhile, outside, Reese opened the car door for Quinn, beginning to prove that he wouldn't hurt her.

"Woww, such a gentleman.", *Quinn teased, secretly super impressed.*

"Not all chivalry is dead.", *He replied.*

"I appreciate that.", *she said with a smile, as she sat in her seat.*

"Something told me you would.", *he shot her a ruggedly cute smile, and gently shut the car door.*

Chapter 6

TELL ME ABOUT IT

Reese and Quinn have been driving for about 15 minutes already, and surprisingly, there's no awkward silence. More surprising than that, they actually have quite a bit in common, but, they still have enough quirks to be different from each other. Both of them have one major passion, music. Turns out, Reese is a fire bass player; he let Quinn go through all his videos, leaving her impressed and somewhat flustered in the best way. She felt competitive, yet, relieved that they shared some common interests.

"So, where are we going anyways?", *Quinn asked with a slight smile.*

"It's a surprise.".

"That's a little sus.", *Quinn teased.*

"Let me guess, you feel the same way about surprises that you do about prom?".

"How do you know how I feel about prom?", *Quinn turned her body, adjusted her seatbelt under her arm, and stared at him with a smirk.*

"I mean, it's not exactly hard to tell; when you walk into school and gag at the promposals.. it's pretty obvious.", *Reese chuckled.*

"Whateverrr.".

"So what happened? Did some guy stand you up on your date as a joke and then crack an egg on your head in the middle of homecoming or something?", *he asked.*

"You just described a bad coming of age movie, not my life.".

"Strict parents?".

"I mean, I barely see my parents so.. it's definitely not that.".

"Oh, I'm sorry, I didn't—

"No, it's fine. It doesn't bother me, I like living with Brylee.".

"So, then what made you so bitter about prom?".

"I'm not bitter about prom. I just don't want to associate myself with prom goers, Brylee not included, just to be clear.".

"Ah, I get it.", *Reese smirked as he pulled into a strangely familiar parking lot.*

"Get what?", *she shot a look at him that could've burned through his body.*

"You're the typical edgy teen who doesn't like to follow the trends; the one in the movies that gets dragged along to pep rallies and proms by their bubbly bestie, just to sit in the corner wearing all black, disinterested at everyone and everything you see.", *Reese put the car in park, raised his eyebrows, and gave Quinn a somewhat smug look.*

"You're wrong.", *Quinn challenged him.*

"Oh, am I?", *Reese playfully chuckled.*

"Mmhm, look at me, the top half of me is sparkly and pink.", *she retorted.*

"Considering that I haven't seen you wear pink, or glitter for that matter all the years I've sat in class with you, I'm gonna go out on a limb and guess that that came out of Brylee's closet; and that she forced you to wear it.".

"Despite your lack of… wrongness—

"You do look absolutely breathtaking though. A rare masterpiece, a once in a lifetime vision that I'm so grateful I get to set my eyes on. I'm sorry I hadn't taken the time to say that to you yet, I should've said it the moment you walked into the living room.. but, I guess I was just trying to build up the courage.".

Quinn bashfully smiled and bit her lip, astounded at his eloquence, his imaginative description, and his perception of her.

"I'm glad you worked up the courage.", *she responded, trying to keep her cool.*

Reese chuckled, unbuckled, and got out of the car; he quickly made his way around to Quinn, opened her door, and extended his hand to help her out.

"If I'm so wrong about you, you're just gonna have to prove it, Q-tip.", *he winked and smiled as he helped her out of the car.*

"Oh, I will.", *Quinn answered him, intrigued by his keen sense of character.*

Once she was out of the car, Reese gently, yet, firmly, grabbed her hand, guided her away from the car and shut her door. He switched sides with her, casually grabbing her other hand, making sure that he was facing the side with traffic. They began walking and suddenly his trunk popped open.

"You didn't tell me where we were going, and now your trunk is open in a parking lot. You aren't helping your case, Newb.", *Quinn poked at him.*

"If you think that's sus, you're not gonna like what I have to say next. Close your eyes.", *Reese confidently demanded.*

"You're right, now it sounds like the beginning of a 'True Crime' podcast.".

"Just do it.", *Reese playfully sighed.*

Quinn crossed her arms and closed her eyes as Reese ruffled around his trunk.

"You know, I wouldn't be an easy hostage. I could annoy you like you would not believe!", *Quinn rambled.*

Tell Me About It

"Oh, don't worry, I totally believe it.".

Quinn smiled, reached out and (playfully) smacked Reese as she heard him giggling at his own joke.

"Okay, open your eyes.", *he said with a wide smile.*

Quinn opened her eyes to see him standing there holding two guitars.

"What are those for?", *she asked.*

"Well, they're generally used to make this thing called music, but, I suppose we could use them as plates while we eat.".

"Ha ha, nice sarcasm.", *Q playfully crossed her arms and raised her eyebrows.*

"Okay, okay, I'm sorry. I was gonna take you bowling, but, the more we talked, I thought you'd enjoy this more.".

"How do you know I can even play?".

"C'mon, do you honestly think I haven't made it to one of your gigs before?".

'He's come to one of my shows? I can't believe I didn't notice him. Did he think I was good? Why do I feel so comfortable with him? It's like I've known him forever… oh no! What if he can read my thoughts?! Pizza. Music. Brylee. Sleep.", Quinn's thoughts piled up as if the random things she came up with would push out her deeper, more vulnerable ones. She acted like she was clearing out her brain's search history.

"I know it doesn't look like much from out here, but it's pretty epic inside.", *Reese reassured her as they approached the door.*

"Okay, but if it's wack and boring, I get to choose where we go next time.", *Quinn teased.*

"'Next time', huh?", *Reese smiled as he twirled Q around and opened the door for her.*

She didn't give him an answer, but she gave him a beautifully mysterious smile, as she walked through the door. This time, she took his hand, and he followed. The inside of the building looked just as dull and lifeless as the outside, maybe even more rundown if possible. It seemed like a horrendous place for a date, especially a first date. Reese quickly took back control and lead her to the cashier's stand.

"Hey, top of the mornin'.", *he confidently nodded to the "cashier".*

Q looked at him with a confused demeanor; before she could ask any questions, the guy behind the counter waved them back.

"Alright, ready for the good part?", *Reese asked as he motioned to pick her up.*

"Woah.. what are you doing?", *Quinn questioned.*

"I was gonna help you hop the counter, it's the only way through.", *he innocently explained.*

"You've never seen me in my kitchen at 6:30 a.m. and it shows.", *Q effortlessly hoisted herself up onto the counter and slid over it gracefully.*

"Yeah, well, I'm trying to change that.", *Reese used one hand to steady himself on the counter, and suddenly threw all his body weight over it; his jump looked even more flawless than hers.*

"It's not a competition.", *she nudged.*

"But, if it was, I'd win.", *he winked and once again began leading her through another door.*

"Hopefully the last one is better than the first two.", *she mumbled.*

"Okay, just keep walking forward until I say stop.", *he reached from behind and placed his hands over her eyes.*

She slowly walked forward for what felt like forever, until, finally, he said stop, and she felt a cold puff of air. She opened her eyes and saw blue, red, and purple lights; about 12 tables and a full crowd. The place looked rustic and retro, yet modern; it was exactly the place she hoped her first date would be.

"Surprise!", *Reese softly exclaimed,* "Do you like it? If not, we can go.".

Q looked up at him, smiled, and took one of his guitars.

"A girl after my own heart.", he thought to himself.

Quinn put the guitar strap around her and started strumming. A familiar, soft rock, tune started effortlessly flying from the strings, almost better than the original.

"No way, you know 'Blue Thunder'?!", *he asked, surprised.*

It was an underground band that only had 13,000 listeners.

"First song I learned.".

"You know the words too?".

"What kind of question is that?", *she answered while biting her lip and staring intently at her own playing.*

"Bet. I'll be right back.".

"Okay.", *she retorted without even batting an eye, then suddenly she realized what he said,* "Wait, where are you going?".

Reese rushed up on stage and claimed the lonely mic.

"Excuse me, everyone.", *he cleared his throat,* "How about some entertainment?".

The crowd started cheering, and Quinn couldn't help but smile and look up at him in wonder and amazement.

"We have a VERY special lady here tonight.", *he found her with his eyes and smiled at her, making her blush.* "She's somewhat of a local celebrity, so let's welcome MS. QUINN DARCY up to the stage!", *he announced as he started clapping and waving her up.*

Quinn made her way on stage and took over the mic.

"And, please welcome my amazing, and kinda cute bass player, MR. REESE SPENCER!", *she copied his announcement, looked at him, smiled and winked just like he does.*

His heart melted, this girl was everything he'd ever dreamed of and more. The audience cheered louder as they got hooked up to their amps.

"You guys know any 'Blue Thunder'?", *Quinn shouted excitedly to the crowd. The moment they cheered, Reese started playing.*

As Reese and Quinn were living their dream at some underground hangout, Brylee was refraining from blowing up her phone about every detail of her very uneventful night.

"It's been hourssss!!!", *Brylee groaned, while hanging half way off the couch.*

"Honey, it's been two and a half hours. You've got to take your mind off of Quinn.", *her mom reminded her.*

"How many times is acceptable to text her while she's gone?", *Bry asked.*

"Five.", *her dad answered almost as soon as she asked the question.*

Brylee let out a relieved smile.

"Three!", *her mom snapped.*

"Three?! But, she's gone for five hours!!", *Bryan frantically responded.*

"You're worse than Bry! Guy's, she's almost 18!! We have to trust her and give her a chance; she'll text if something's wrong, she knows her curfew, the boy she's with seems respectful and responsible. Plus! Have you ever known her to allow herself to be pushed around or taken advantage of?! NOO! You'd be better off wondering if Reese is doing okay. Now, calm down you two!", *KaraLee exclaimed.*

"How are you so calm and collected, mom?", *Brylee asked.*

"Because, I have to be.", *she replied, as she left to get her third cup of coffee.*

Brylee and her dad looked at each other and shrugged.

To: Q

"Hey, how's it going? Consider this text number one btw.". 5:00 p.m.

delivered

"You do realize that technically, according to mom's logic, we can send her six messages, combined..", *Bryan said sneakily, while smirking at Bry.*

"I like the way you think, dad.. I like the way you think.", *she leaned over and high-fived him.*

"That can't be good.", KaraLee thought to herself.

Suddenly, there was a strong knock at the door.

"SHE"S HOME!", *KaraLee shouted.*

Brylee and her dad both looked at her.

"I mean, Honey, get the door.", *she tried to collect herself.*

"Why wouldn't she be using her key? Plus, she said she'd text me when she was on her way home.", *Brylee hesitantly asked.*

"Maybe she forgot.", *Bryan nonchalantly replied.*

"She may have forgotten to text, but I handed her her key when she hugged me on the way out the door.", *Bry assured her parents.*

"For goodness sake you two, I guess I'll get the door.", *her mom cut in.*

KaraLee walked over to the door and looked out the peephole.

"Brylee, sweetheart, are you expecting anyone?", *her mom asked.*

"Yeah, Quinn.", *she dryly replied.*

Kara glared at her as her eyes asked, "Perhaps anyone else?".

"Reese?".

Her mom shot her a look that read, "I'm done with your sarcasm.". They heard the knock again, this time more aggressively.

"He's a handsome young man. Tall, blonde, thin, brown eyes it looks like. Any of this ring a bell?", *KaraLee described.*

"Mom, you just described Justin Bieber, and no, I'm not expecting any—

Visible panic crept onto Brylee's face.

"What's the matter, honey?", *her dad asked with concern laced through his tone.*

"Do you know him?", *her mom quizzed her.*

Brylee stayed frozen, running through her and Jason's earlier conversation, and thinking about how Quinn NEEDED *to be here with her now.*

"I think she's probably just upset about Quinn, he's probably taking surveys or something, just open the door.", *Bryan demanded.*

Brylee attempted to say, "No, don't!", but it was too late, her mom already had the door wide open. Bry quickly threw a blanket over herself and began texting Quinn.

To: Q

"Q! I'm so sorry, I know you're on a date, and I don't want to distract you or worry you, so don't freak out, but, Jason is here! Please text me back when you have a chance!".

Meanwhile, Quinn and Reese just finished their set, and are sitting at a table, sharing fries.

"Two messages from 'B', she's probably just checking up on me, I'll text her when we leave.", *Quinn thought to herself.*

Just then, a husky man approached their table, exuding unbreakable confidence.

"I was watching you two kids from the audience, and I thought I'd come over and introduce myself.", *the man announced,* "My name is, JT Walker, as in —

"As in Walker Records?!", *Quinn quietly exclaimed.*

Reese just smiled along, not having a single clue as to who this guy was, or what "Walker Records" was.

"That's exactly right, Little Lady.", *the man kindly chuckled to himself, and reached out to shake both of their hands.*

"Forgive me, but, I guess I'm a little unfamiliar with you and your record label, Mr. Walker.", *Reese admitted,* "I must not be as caught up on the trends as my girl here.", *he teased, knowing that she'd roll her eyes.*

"Well, I suppose I'm only trendy in the underground arenas, I'm the one who made 'Blue Thunder' the underground stars that they are today. I heard your covers up there, and you sir play a mean bass. It pairs perfectly with your girlfriend's unique, raspy voice. You guys really have somethin', lots of chemistry for sure.", *he smirked at them.*

"Thank you, but, I'm not his girlfriend.", *Quinn chuckled and corrected him.*

"Yet.", *Reese smirked at Q.*

Chapter 7

DONUTS AND DECISIONS

It's 9:45 p.m., Quinn has been back for about 50 minutes, long enough for her to ask all her Jason related questions, and for Brylee to explain what happened while she was gone.

"I can't believe that happened. Are you okay?", *Quinn asked with great concern.*

"I'm fine, it was just surreal and terrifying. I mean, how did he get my address?!", *Brylee exclaimed, still in shock.*

"I don't know… we need to find that out, but, in the meantime, what do we do? Do your parents know what happened between you two?".

"No.. I just told them we used to be friends..", *Brylee shyly admitted.*

"Used to be friends!?", *Quinn shouted with wide eyes, in disbelief.*

"I didn't want to worry them.", *she admitted.*

"They're your parents! It's their jobbb!!!", *Q insisted.*

"They were already all worried about you.".

"So? They're your parents! That's their jobbb!!!!", *Quinn clapped as she shouted.*

Just then, Brylee's parents walked into her room to see what all the shouting was about.

"Quinnyyyyy..", *Bryan teased,* "How was your big date!!?".

Quinn blushed, and fought her giggling until it forced its way out.

"So it was good, I presume.", *KaraLee said with a smile.*

"Quinn! We've been so busy talking about me, I haven't even heard about your date!", *Brylee exclaimed, hoping to distract her friend from her problems.*

"You, Brylee Brown, haven't heard about your best friend's FIRST date, yet? She's been home for like an hour.", *Bryan questioned her, surprised.*

"Something must be seriously wrong here.", *KaraLee sarcastically joked.*

"Well, actually..", *Quinn looked at her best friend with a stare that demanded she confess.*

"Bry-Bry, are you okay?", *her dad asked.*

Brylee began tearing up as Quinn started moving her hand up and down her upper-back in support.

"It's okay, B, go ahead.", *Q encouraged her.*

"Okay, you're starting to scare us, Brylee, what's going on?", *KaraLee hesitantly demanded an answer.*

Brylee grabbed her phone, opened photos, and handed it to her parents.

"Read the screenshots. That's my conversation with the boy who showed up earlier.", *she explained.*

A few minutes passed as her parents read the screenshots, Quinn had her hand resting on Brylee's shoulder, to comfort her, while she was trying to control her breathing. As she held back tears, she glanced up at her worried parents, with glassy eyes and a turning stomach. Once they both finished reading they regained their composure, handed their daughter back her phone, and looked compassionately into her eyes.

"I'll step outside so you guys can have her all to yourselves.", *Quinn humbly offered.*

"No!", *Brylee snapped up and grabbed her hand,* "Please stay, I need really need you right now.".

Quinn looked up at her friend's parents as if she was asking if it was alright.

"Quinny, don't be silly, you're family, stay.", *Bryan assured her.*

"Yeah, I'm sure my Brylee needs you more than ever right now, this is a scary situation.", *KaraLee followed,* "Why didn't you tell us yesterday, sweetheart?".

"I didn't wanna worry you guys over something that was probably nothing.".

"Sweetheart, worry us about whatever you want; we don't care if it's big or small, we want to know, we want to help. If I would've known you had this conversation in the first place, I would've advised you not to egg this guy on, I mean, he's clearly unstable.", *her mom continued.*

"I'm sorry. So, what do I do?".

Bryan and KaraLee looked at each-other to confirm what each of them was thinking.

"Honey, you're gonna have to file a restraining order against this guy.", *her dad responded.*

"Well, this escalated quickly.", *Quinn mumbled under her breath.*

"You're right, Quinn, it did escalate quickly; and because it's escalated to this point so quickly, I think you need to take precaution, Bry-Bry. In fact, there's no question about it, you're going to file one. I know you're almost an adult, but, you're still my little girl, and I need to make sure you're safe, especially with all the going out you're getting ready to do, both of you girls. It might seem a little crazy right now, but he's shown himself to be, well… crazy; there's consequences for actions, this is his.", *Bryan explained.*

KaraLee nodded in agreement, and Brylee stared at Quinn waiting for a look of confirmation; once she got it, she began to speak.

"Okay, I'll do it; you're right.", *Brylee perked up a bit,* "What about the threat I made to expose him? Do I follow through with that? I mean, shouldn't those other girls know what they're getting themselves into?", *she quizzed her parents.*

"Yes, they should know, and we'll figure something out; but I don't want it connected to you. Our first priority is you girls, and your safety; once we secure that, we'll put something out for the others.", *Bryan explained.*

"Okay, I understand.", *Bry replied, slightly disappointed in his answer.*

"Good.", *KaraLee stepped in,* "You know this isn't your fault, right, Honey?".

"Thanks, I really needed to hear that.", *Brylee replied softly, with a slight smile.*

KaraLee and Bryan walked over and hugged the girls tightly.

"We love you both more than you know.", *KaraLee lovingly gazed into both of their eyes,* "I'm talking to you too, Quinn, you're one of us, that's why it feels so weird when you visit your parents; you complete this little family, and I wouldn't have it any other way.".

Quinn smiled and began to tear up.

"I might have you slightly quieter, but other than that, I agree.", *Bryan teased to lighten up the mood.*

Quinn sniffled, wiped her eyes, and laughed along with the family.

"Now, your date! Tell me EVERYTHING!!!", *Brylee excitedly hollered.*

"Alright, we'll give you girls some privacy, there's donuts in the kitchen if you want them. I know you talk about all your major life moments over donuts, I figured this was one of them.", *Bryan shared.*

"Thanks, Dad.", *Bry said with a soft smile.*

"Love you guys!!", *the girls shouted as Bry's parents left the room.*

"Okay! Tell meeee!", *B insisted.*

"I can't.", *Quinn dryly replied.*

"What? Why not??", *her friend roared.*

"Because, there's no donut in my hand.".

Brylee rolled her eyes and teasingly scoffed as she jumped up from her bed.

"I will get you donuts since you're probably tired from all the flirting, but then, no more distractions, you're going to tell me every last detail!", *she demanded.*

"Deal.", *Quinn chuckled.*

Bry raced out of the bedroom, swiftly snatched the box of donuts off the counter and her feet quickly pitter pattered back to their room.

Chapter 8

WHAT DO I DO?

It's 6 a.m., the sun is barely shining through their curtains, and Brylee is awakened by the never-ending clicking of Quinn's text keyboard.

"*Groans.*".

"Goodmorninggg sleepyhead, when am I ever awake before you?", *Quinn excitedly remarked.*

"*Groans.*".

"I've been awake for like an hour. I woke up all jittery for some reason; like a kid on Christmas Eve. It's weird waking up and seeing you in bed instead of holding my coffee.", *Q trailed on with all the energy in the world.*

"Glad to be assistant to you.", *Brylee tiredly grumbled, half asleep.*

"Don't you mean, 'of assistance'?".

"No, I don't need assistance; I need sleep.".

"This feels like one of those bank calls. Like when you call the 800-number to talk about anything other than the keypad choices, so you have to talk to the automated guy, and he keeps telling you to repeat yourself.", *Quinn expressed.*

Brylee grumbled in slight frustration while shoving her face into her pillow, however, she quickly came to terms with the fact that she was up so early on a Sunday, and chose to make the best of it, despite the night she had. She decided that she'd rather feel love in the air than anything else, and realized how incredibly happy she was for her best friend. After she took in everything going on, and became slightly more awake, she popped up, wrapped herself in her blanket, and faced toward Quinn, who had a permanent smile on her face.

"So, how's it goin' with Reese?".

"Oh, I don't know..", *Quinn's smile grew larger,* "It's only been a couple days.".

"That's not what I asked.".

Quinn set her phone down, looked up at Bry, smiled, and let out a happy sigh. You could clearly see how euphoric she was feeling.

"Ah, to be walking on air.", *Brylee poked.*

"Is it that obvious?", *Quinn asked, slightly embarrassed.*

"The only thing that would make it clearer is if your heart-filled haze visibly formed and followed you around.", *she smiled,* "But, that's how it's supposed to be.".

"I can't help it! I really like him, but, I don't know all the rules! Do I ask him out next? Do I wait for him to ask? Are we dating? Will he ask me to be his girlfriend? And, most importantly, HOW DID I GET LIKE THIS?!".

"You got it, you got it bad..", *Bry started singing.*

"B!", *Quinn explained.*

"Okay, okay. Don't get caught up in all the, 'rules', you guys need your own set of rules. In the meantime, there is no rule about who asks who out, or the time in-between. He's probably wondering the same exact thing right now; if you wanna go for it, then go for it. If you'd rather wait, then wait; I'm confident that he'll ask you out again, soon.", *Brylee assured her.*

"You always know exactly what to say.".

"I don't know about that..".

Bry was clearly still nervous about filling out the restraining order.

"Is this about the RO?", *Quinn carefully asked.*

"RO?".

"Restraining order.", *Quinn muttered.*

"Oh.. yeah, no! It's not, I'm great!".

Quinn gave Bry a glare that made her spill her guts.

"Okay, yes! Because like, what if I'm overreacting?! Did I gaslight him?! What if the police tell me I'M wrong???? I don't know how this works. Did I build this all up in my head?! Am I about to ruin this guy's life over prom???", *Brylee began to hyperventilate as she confessed.*

"Bry! Calm down! You're gonna send yourself into a full blown panic attack if you don't take control right now! Breathe with me.", *Quinn exclaimed.*

Q took a steady, deep breath in and Bry followed suit. They practiced her inhale/exhale exercise until her heart rate stabilized; once she was calm, Quinn started talking.

"Okay, first things first, you certainly aren't ruining his life. The only people who know about the restraining order are your families and the cops, as long as you guys don't tell anyone else, okay?", *Quinn reassured her.*

Brylee nodded as a sign that she understood.

"Good. Now, second of all, you didn't make all this up. You didn't build it up in your head, I've seen the messages, and if that's not enough, your parents did too. You made it PERFECTLY clear that you were uninterested, and that fool straight up stalked you and found your house, then CAME TO IT. He is the only one gaslighting, and the only life getting ruined is gonna be yours if you don't do this, or some unsuspecting girl if we don't tell the truth about Jason. Remember what he did while he was here, it was sick, twisted, and it'll only get worse. The only person making things up in their head is him.", *Q defended her.*

"Yeah, you're right. Thank you, I don't know what I'd do without you, Q.", *Bry softly smiled at her and formed heart hands.*

"I love you, dude, always. Now, can we get some coffee and Talk about Reese? I really hope that didn't sound selfish.".

"You're the least selfish person I know, go for it!".

"Alright, cool, let me—

Quinn was interrupted by the chime of her school email.

"Is that school? I thought they stopped sending emails last month? I haven't gotten any.", *Bry asked.*

"Yeah.. I thought so too, hopefully it's not about what I said in class..", *Q dove right into her email to make sure she didn't get suspended before graduation.* "Uh oh.".

"What?!".

"It's from Vice Principal Peterssss..", *Quinn moaned.*

"What does it say??", *Brylee quizzed.*

"I can't open it!", *Q blurted,* "You do it!", *she threw her phone at her best friend, and wrapped herself around her pillow like a koala bear.*

Softly giggling, Brylee opened the email and began to read aloud. She assumed a terribly fake British accent, while announcing the letter as if she was making a royal decree.

"Dear Ms. Quinn Darcy, I'm very pleased to announce that despite your somewhat angsty reports, you'll be graduating as the top student in our school..", *Brylee switched back to her normal accent as she continued to read,* "You've achieved the highest test scores our school has seen yet, and in record time, too! I'm pleased to present you as one of two nominees for valedictorian!! Of course, we'll have to choose between the two *existing candidates, but, this is a no-brainer. I'm confident that you will take the cake! Best wishes, Vice Principal Peters.".*

Bry faked a smile and congratulated her as she handed Quinn her phone; but immediately after the exchange, she sat there dazed.

"Well, obviously I'm going to delete this, we all know you were made to be valedictorian.", *Quinn tried making her feel better, while assuring her she didn't want to take her spotlight.*

"No! Don't delete it, you should be proud of yourself! Call your parents! Oh, and tell Reese! He'll definitely be impressed.", *Bry babbled, clearly troubled.*

"Right, anyways, TRASH!", *Quinn exclaimed as she pressed delete.*

"Quinn, don't be ridiculous. Don't throw away the most important thing that's ever happened to you.".

"VD is definitely not the most important thing to ever happen to me. The most important thing to happen to my parents maybe, not me.".

"Quinn, don't—

Quinn cut her off, tired of arguing about a pointless subject.

"Bry! Stop. Something far more important happened to me last night, and I wasn't ready to say anything, but now, I am.".

"HE PROMPOSED!", *Brylee excitedly assumed.*

"No.".

"He proposed?", *she sarcastically questioned.*

"Dude, can I talk?".

"Sorry. Go ahead.".

"Reese and I did our set..".

"Right, dream come true, you went on about it.".

"Right, yeah. Then after the show we were chillin' at a table together, and this guy approached us.".

"Oh no, don't tell me you have to file a restraining order too. I mean, twinsies, get it I guess.".

"He was Mr. Walker of Walker Studios!!!", *Q shouted.*

"As in, 'Blue Thunder', Walker Studios, Mr. Walker?!", *Bry excitedly asked.*

Quinn nodded, waiting for the info to truly sink into her friend.

"HE OFFERED YOU A DEAL, DIDN'T HE?!".

"He wants Reese and I to record a whole album with him; then after graduation, he wants to set us up on a mini tour which is like 25 out-of-state gigs.", *Q explained.*

"So, how long does a mini tour last?".

"Two months, I think.".

"Two months without you.. that's sad, but it could be worse. I'm really happy for you. Man, a boyfriend and a career all at once, when you try something new you really just go for it, huh?", *Brylee teased.*

"You can come too, ya know, it's during summer so you don't have to take a year off if you don't want to. We can make it home in time to get ready for fall semester. Plus, I think I might have a better opportunity if you come, no way your parents or mine will let me go on tour alone with a boy.".

"Okay, alright, let me process… yes! I accept your offer! This is gonna be the best summer ever! Maybe we'll get introduced to Blue Thunder!!!".

"Woah, girl, hold your horses. I don't know about all that chief, but, we need to talk to your parents first. If they agree, so will mine.".

"You're right. I think we need to ask after this whole restraining order thing though. If we worry them about two major things at once, I'm not so sure they'll see this as a great opportunity like we do.".

"Yeah, I was thinking the same. Speaking of, we need to get dressed and eat, cuz your dad said he wants to get there as soon as they open. They open in twenty minutes.".

"Already?!".

"It's gonna be okay. Don't be nervous, I'll be with you the whole time.".

The girls got up, brushed their teeth, threw their hair in messy buns, slipped into their favorite sweatpants and baggy tees, did their skincare; then, made their way into the kitchen with five minutes to spare.

"Good morning, my beautiful girls.", *Bryan greeted them.*

"Morning, Mr. B!", *Quinn replied.*

"Hey, dad.", *Bry followed.*

"How you holdin' up, Bry-Bry?", *he asked in an empathetic tone.*

"I'm hungry.".

"Same.", *Quinn chimed in while looking through the pantry.*

"Lucky for you girls, after this thing is over with, I'm taking you out to breakfast.", *Bryan remarked cheerfully,* "Just grab a donut to hold you over until we're done at the station.".

"Oh, you got more donuts, Mr. B?".

"No, the ones from last night, Quinny.".

"Those are long gone, dad.", *Bry revealed.*

"No way.", *he looked at Quinn in disbelief.*

"Way. You handed two girls handling two different, somewhat stressful situations a dozen donuts to keep us company while we talked.".

"They were gone within an hour.", *Brylee looked at her dad.*

"Women never cease to amaze me.", *Bryan retorted.*

The girls smirked and high-fived each-other.

"What if I get you coffee on the way? Will that hold you till—

Before Bryan could finish his sentence, the girls had his keys and were heading out the door.

"Coffee. Remember that, Bryan, coffee shuts them up.", *he chuckled to himself as he followed them out.*

Chapter 9

BAILIFFS AND BREAKFAST

Bryan got the girls their coffee and some scones, and made it to the police station with 10 minutes to spare. They've been sitting in the station's parking lot for 7 minutes, waiting for it to open.

"It's almost time to go in, should we have a count down?", *Quinn pointed out.*

"I'd rather not.", *Bry replied.*

"It's okay Bry-Bry, thousands of people file these daily. It's just a safety precaution. Quinn and I will be with you every step of the way, and your mom will meet us at breakfast.", *Bryan reassured her.*

"Thanks, dad.".

Brylee laid her head on her dad's shoulder as she sipped her iced coffee.

"Is it considered littering if my scone happens to make a second appearance on the sidewalk out there?", *B said, somewhat sarcastically.*

Quinn popped up from the backseat so that she was resting in between the driver and passenger seats.

"Hum. I've heard humming helps with nausea bro.", *Quinn explained.*

"And just in case, I'd lay off that coffee for now, I'll buy you more at the restaurant, when this is over.", *Bryan demanded,* "Here.".

Bryan handed his daughter a stick of gum, and nodded for her to chew it.

"Mint, that helps too.", *Quinn chimed.*

"Want some, Quinny?".

"Is that your way of telling me I have coffee breath, Mr. B?".

"Like I said, want some, Quinny?".

"Hint taken.", *Quinn retorted as she snatched the stick of gum he was holding up.*

"Okay, guys, they've been open for 7 minutes already, should we go in and get this over with?", *Brylee nervously inquired.*

"Let's go.", *her dad breathed.*

Bryan and Brylee got out of the car, meanwhile, Quinn was knocking on the window. Bryan chuckled and opened her door.

"I still don't see why you haven't taken the child lock off, Mr. B.", *Q squinted.*

"Ah, yes, the mystery remains.", *he teased.*

Bryan put his arm around Brylee's shoulder to comfort her as all three walked into the entrance.

"Here we go.", *Brylee exhaled to herself as she put her nausea on pause.*

As they walked through the doors into the bitter-cold lobby, the smell of stale, black coffee engulfed them. There were dull, black benches against the wall to the right, and the waiting room was complete with a water dispenser. You just knew everything in there was beyond filthy, who knows what perp left what bodily fluid behind on those seats. Standing was the only logical option. Aside from the cops, the only other living thing near us was a fern in the corner; wait a minute, it looks waxy, it's probably a fake. I felt cold stares of judgment coming from the officers, who knew a police station would feel so much like a high school classroom; I mean, seriously, what could they possibly be judging right now? This does not make me feel better about filling out the RO, what if they think I'm faking? Do they call on us like the deli guy, or do we go up? Is this self-serve like a buffet? Is there a mailer full of documents I can grab and drop off?

"Brylee, steady your breathing, sweetheart, you have nothing to worry about. Why don't you stay here with Q, I'll go talk to that woman over there, and see what we do from here.", *Bryan assured her.*

Bry nodded in agreement and took several deep breaths; Quinn joined her as she grabbed her hand in support.

"We're here, Bry, you just have to give an account of what happened. It's just like telling a story, it just has to be non-fiction.", *Quinn poked, in an attempt to soothe her friend's nerves.*

Brylee giggled in relief.

"You're right. Thanks for always being there, Q.", *she squeezed Quinn's hand.*

Just then, Bryan walked back over to the girls with a very soft smile on his face.

"Oh no..", *Brylee sharply sighed.*

"Your dad's bad news face.".

"Okay, so, it's no big deal, but—

"But.", *Bry cut off her dad,* "All good news starts with, 'but'.".

"It's not bad. You just have to go up there and tell her about the other night, she's very kind. She knows you're nervous, and is ready to help you any way she can.", *her dad assured her.*

"So, what's the catch, Mr. B?".

"Well, Quinn and I have to stay in the waiting area so they can be sure that we aren't coaching you, swaying you, or feeding you a story of our own. It makes sense. We'll be right back here, silently cheering you on; you've got this!", *Bryan tried to be confident.*

Bailiffs and Breakfast

Brylee quickly grew pale and woozy, as she started to hyperventilate.

"Deep breaths, Bry-Bry.", *Bryan gently coached.*

Suddenly, Quinn flicked her, which distracted her from the situation, and mildly took Bryan by surprise.

"Snap out of it! You've got this!", *Quinn put her hands on B's shoulders,* "Go, tattle-tale on Jason, in detail, and come back here so we can celebrate with food and more coffee!", *Quinn encouraged.*

Without saying a word, Brylee turned around and briskly walked to the counter where the woman was waiting for her. Quinn and Bryan looked at each-other.

"I don't know if you upset her, or gave her the push she needed; whatever you did, it worked.".

Quinn smirked as if to say, "I know my best friend.", *then proceeded to drape herself across one of the benches. Bryan quickly followed suit, and took a seat while he watched the encounter take place.*

"Hello, Ms. Brylee.".

The woman cordially greeted her with a smile, as she made her way to the window.

"Hello, Mrs. D.", *Brylee shakily read the woman's name tag.*

"Call me Dianne.", *she motioned for Brylee to take a seat.*

"So, I don't really know what to do here. Do I just start telling you, or?".

"Well, actually, I'll guide the conversation, you don't have to worry about a thing. I'll start by asking you for some of your information, and whatever you can give me on this guy.", *Dianne explained.*

"Okay, sounds easy enough.", *Brylee squeaked as she bit the inside of her cheek.*

"Alright, sweetheart, date of birth?", *Dianne began quizzing.*

"July 5, 2004.".

"How exciting! Your birthday is coming up so soon, the big 18, I see.", Mrs. D *winked at her,* "The day after the 4th of July too, I bet you're a little firecracker, babygirl.".

The way Dianne spoke, the little jokes she told, and the names of endearment she called a complete stranger, made the process much less scary.

"I'd like to think so.", *Brylee giggled in response.*

"Full name?".

"Brylee Hannah Brown.".

"Hannah. I love that, it's my sister's name. Okay, lastly, in a word or two, can you tell me why you'd like to file this restraining order?".

"Well, I guess I'd say harassment.", *she sheepishly admitted.*

"Mmm, no, baby, I don't think so.", *Dianne started, her choice of words made Brylee's heart-rate skyrocket; however, it quickly came down as Mrs. D finished her sentence,* "Nobody harasses Ms. Brylee and gets away with it. Mrs. D gotchu honey.".

A soft smile of relief crept across Bry's face.

"Okay, so, do you think you can answer some basic questions about this icky boy?", *Dianne became very animated as she scrunched her nose, and forced a bitter beer expression onto her face.".*

"I'll try my best.".

"Okay, baby, what's his name?".

"Jason McKinley.".

"Do you know his birthday?".

"July 8, 2003.".

Bailiffs and Breakfast

"Well, he's the wrong kind of firecracker now isn't he.", *Dianne mumbled to herself as she gave her computer the information it demanded,* "Can you give me a description? Be as specific as you can, please.".

"Sure. He's tall, Caucasian, probably around 6'1" or 6'2". He has dark blonde hair, parted in the middle, tapered at the ear. His eyes are chocolate brown. He has very strong facial features; prominent cheekbones, and jawline. Unmistakable. He dresses preppy, I don't know if that helps.", *she confessed.*

"Any little bit helps, honey, does this boy drive?".

"Yes, he does.".

"Do you know what kind of vehicle?".

"I don't know the make and model, I just know that he drives a blue, topless, jeep.".

"Okay, that's perfect. So, before I ask you to tell me what happened, I'm going to explain what this process looks like. I also need you to sign a paper which states that you haven't been coached, you aren't making this up, you haven't been deemed 'crazy' in a U.S. court of law, etc.".

"Okay, sounds good, I'm ready.".

"Okay, Brylee, this is a protective order. That means, the court will order this Jason to stay away from you for a set period of time. After that time runs out, you'll have to extend it, that is, if you still feel the need to have it in place. Are you with me so far?".

"Yes, I understand.".

"Okay, good. Secondly, this does have to be taken to court because a judge has to put it in place. This step seems scary, but, it's perfectly normal; since you filed with me, I will be the bailiff on call, so I will be seeing your sweet face once again. Still with me?".

"Yes, I'm sorry, I just didn't realize we had to go to court.".

"That's how serious this is, honey. We have to walk you through the procedures, that way, if you weren't serious about this, you could walk out with a warning; false accusations are punishable by the court of law, and this always weeds them out. I can see the sincerity in your eyes, baby, so I'm just helping you understand the next steps. Ready for me to continue?".

"Yes, ma'am.".

"Alright. Although you can do this on your own, I suggest you retain an attorney. I can recommend you a few, good, affordable options; I'll send you home with a packet so you and your parents can make a decision that's best for you.".

Brylee nodded along as Dianne explained procedure, however, she wasn't really there anymore. All she could think about was court. Intrusive thoughts telling her that she was being too extreme pelted her until finally she made the choice to take control of her mind. By the time she snapped out of it, Dianne was finished.

"Does this all make sense, sweetheart?".

"Uh, yes. Yeah! It does, thank you.".

"It's my job, baby. All this information will be repeated in the packet I mentioned earlier, so don't worry if you didn't grasp it right away. Now, I have to ask, do you still want to continue?".

Bry took a deep breath, and looked back at Quinn, searching for just a shred of support. She saw Quinn silently cheering, pumping her fists, and giving her two thumbs up; while her dad shot her the most comforting smile.

"Okay, yes. I can do this, I would—please— like to continue, Dianne.".

"Okay, baby, this is the hardest easy part. You just have to tell me what happened, take your time.".

"So, first of all, for some background, I have these printed screenshots from the conversation that started it all. Do I give these to you?", *Brylee stammered.*

"Yes! I love a girl who comes prepared. I'll take those, Honey.".

Bry handed off the papers, and Dianne began reading. Her thoughts were on display, thanks to her facial expressions.

"Alright, Ms. Brylee, I am so sorry that this happened. How about you tell me what happened as a result of this.".

"This is the first time I've told anyone, besides my best friend.", *she confessed.*

"Is that her over there?".

Brylee smiled.

"Yep, that's Quinn.".

"I can tell you two have a strong bond. I see her over there cheering you on; friendships like that are true gems. I know I'm not Quinn, but, I promise to be free of judgment, just like a friend should be.", *Dianne assured her.*

"Okay.", *she softly smiled and sat up straight,* "Do you have the date, or do I need to recount all those details?".

"I have the little details, you just go ahead and tell me what happened.".

"Okay, so, Quinn was gone, she had been gone for about two hours at this point. She had her very first date, and I was nervous even though the guy seems amazing and absolutely perfect for her. Pretty much, Quinn was the only thing on my mind.".

Dianne nodded along and intently listened as she typed little notes.

"My dad and I were plotting, trying to plan a way to spam text her while she was on her date; we had to do that because my mom said we should trust Quinn, and only text her three times. While we were conducting our plan, someone knocked. My mom looked through the peep-hole and described the visitor, but, I was so preoccupied, I didn't realize that she was describing Jason, until it was too late. I hadn't told my parents what happened because I thought it was no big deal, so, they wouldn't have guessed it either.

When she opened the door, I hid under a blanket and started texting Quinn. Again, I was preoccupied so I couldn't defend myself, and apparently he introduced himself as one of my friends, and my prom date. My mom was so excited, she invited him in and my dad pulled the blanket off of me. I was forced to interact with him, I was frozen, and my stomach was turning; I didn't even think to tell my parents what happened, so I just awkwardly lived through it.

I was standoffish, so my parents probably just thought I was nervous about a boy; I admit, that wouldn't be unusual for Brylee Brown. He came, sat by me, then put his arm around me. He and my dad chatted for a bit, he fakes it well, he acted like a perfect gentleman, so my parents stepped away to let us talk.

He threatened me. He told me if I didn't go to prom with him I'd regret it, then he scooted closer. He said that he didn't want the other hundred girls he bragged about, he had his eye on me; and he said, no matter how hard I try, I can't get rid of him, after that, he gently swept my hair behind my ear. He then, in great detail, described how he couldn't wait to see me in the dress I bought; but, I never told him about it, so the only way he'd know all those details would be if he was a stalker. Which, he kinda is, I mean, HOW DID HE GET MY ADDRESS?!".

As this became more real to her, she started tearing up.

"It's okay, Baby, keep going, you're doing good.", *Dianne reassured her.*

Quinn heard B raise her voice, and was ready to jump up and save her; Bryan had to calm her down, and talk her down, before she got herself detained.

"I'm sorry for raising my voice.".

"It's okay, Sugar, I understand, it's a stressful situation. Your friend is up-in-arms too, she might make a good cop.", *she poked, trying to calm Bry down.*

"She's actually a pretty successful musician.", *Bry chuckled.*

"I should've guessed it.", *Mrs. D offered a soft, kind smile.*

"Well, after that, he handed me a corsage that matched my dress, and he left. I threw it away, I was so disgusted, and I stayed in my room until Quinn got home. If it wasn't for her, I wouldn't have even told my parents, and I wouldn't be here right now.".

"That's a true best friend.".

"Yeah, she really is.", *B smiled.*

"And I can see here that you also want to make the other girls aware of Jason's character?".

"Yes, ma'am, they deserve to know before they end up here, or worse.".

"I absolutely agree, Ms. Brylee Brown, and you know what? I can actually send a warning to the school to be emailed to the students, and posted up on and around school grounds. I can also arrange an end of the year police assembly to put a little scare into him. It can't be traced back to you whatsoever; I'll go ahead and do that right now. Don't be surprised if you see me at school next week; we gotta stick together. Somethin' tells me that your friend over there could put a little scare into him, herself.", *Dianne winked.*

"You have no idea.", *Brylee chuckled,* "And, thank you so much, I can sleep better knowing that those other girls will have the information they need to make their decisions.".

"Absolutely. And if my math is correct, Jason is already 18?".

"Yes. He started school on the late round.".

"Okay, well, this just became a matter of adult vs minor harassment. Not only harassment, but stalking. I have all I need here. Sugar, I'm so sorry you had to go through this, but, we will get this handled for you right away. Won't we boys?!", *Dianne raised her voice to the officers behind her.*

"Yes! Of course! Right away, ma'am, top priority!", *they all answered at once.*

"Boys. Am I right?", *D smiled at Brylee.*

Dianne handed Brylee the packet, and her business card complete with her personal phone number.

"If you're having any trouble, you call Mrs. D, day or night. Okay, Baby?", *she demanded.*

"I will, thank you.".

Bry smiled, grabbed her things, and made her way back over to Quinn and her dad. Q immediately hopped off her bench, ran, and tackled her with a hug, as soon as she saw her coming.

"How did it go?! Why'd you yell?", *Quinn quizzed her.*

"Quinny, give her a second to breathe.", *Bryan nonchalantly instructed.* "Anyways, how'd it go?! Are you okay?! Why'd you yell?".

Quinn looked at him almost confused.

"I'm fine, guys. It was really good, Dianne was so kind and helpful; and, I got a little overwhelmed, that's why I raised my voice, but, I snapped out of it.".

Quinn held up her hand for a high-five.

"I'm so proud of you!", *Q squealed.*

"Alright, girls.", *Bryan softly chuckled,* "Should we get out of here?".

The girls looked at each-other, looked at Bryan, looked back at each-other, then deviously smiled.

"More coffee! Round two! More coffee! Round two!", *they chanted in sync.*

As they walked out the door, Bryan looked back at Dianne, laughed, and mouthed, "Thank you."; she nodded and smiled, as he left. Just before the door fully shut, we hear Quinn yelling, "BACONNNN!!!", as she slid across the hood of the car to reach her side.

"Mmkay, maybe no more coffee for you.", *Bryan teased.*

Quinn shot him a look that screamed, "WHYYY?!?!", he shrugged.

"Safety reasons, Quinny. The safety of my car.".

Brylee,—laughing— got into the car, taking in just how amazing her life really is.

Chapter 10

BACK TO SCHOOL

It's Monday morning, the girls have gotten ready, and are already on school grounds. Brylee's "loving life" attitude was dwindling with every step closer to the entrance; as Quinn watched the color drain from her best friend's face, she began to reassure her.

"Okay, dude, remember, no one knows about the restraining order… except for you… and Jason.. and probably the principal… and also your teachers.. and possibly more of the staff.. BUT, no other students know!", *Quinn exclaimed, proud of her reassurance tactics.*

Brylee chuckled, and some color began returning to her cheeks.

"Thanks, Quinn, you're right. No other students know.", *Brylee agreed.*

As they entered the school, the sharp, cold cafeteria air seemed to slap Brylee across the face. She tensed up, made no direct eye contact, and power-walked through the multipurpose room, desperately trying to reach the other end. She felt as though everybody knew, and suddenly, anxiety tried grabbing at her ankles, as to trip her up in front of the whole school. Quinn quickly noticed her breathing picking up pace, and saw a look of panic crawling across her face.

"Brylee, breathe.".

"I am breathing.".

"Control your breathing, like this.", *Quinn demonstrated.*

Brylee followed suit, and took control of her breathing. Just as she calmed down, Jenny Walker, (who wanted to be in charge of the prom committee, but lost out to Brylee) walked by.

"What, are you guys practicing your Lamaze?", *Jenny mocked*, "Oh, wait, by the way, I heard what happened, Brylee, sorry you weren't good enough, but, don't worry, I won't make too many changes to your designs. Bye!", *she added, with a smug smirk, and a fake tone in her sarcastic voice.*

"Wasn't good enough?", Brylee thought to herself, "Did Jason tell her? What did he tell her? Did he tell other people?".

"Snap out of it, Bry!", *Quinn demanded as she snapped her fingers, trying to break her friend's daze.*

"Do you think that was about Jason?", *Brylee asked.*

"No. Probably not. That was just Jenny being Jenny, any other day, you would've just ignored it.".

"I'm genuinely surprised that you did.".

"What? Ignore Jenny?", *Quinn asked.*

"Yeah, usually you light her up.".

"Yeah, well, I've been learning that maybe not everything deserves my attention.".

"I hope this isn't about Reese?", *Brylee said with an inquisitive tone, and concern in her voice.*

"No, not about Reese; just, about distractions. You gotta know what's what.".

Brylee softly smiled, and grabbed Q's hand as to say, "I'm proud of you". Quinn smiled back, and continued walking, leading Bry to their lockers. They quickly got there, unlocked them, and grabbed their books; as they shut their locker doors, they saw Mrs. Shay's face. She seemed to have appeared out of nowhere.

"Wow, Mrs. Shay, 'you have quite the ability to remain sneakily silent'.", *Quinn tested her.*

"Ah, Quinn, and who are you quoting this time? Shakespeare? Elton John? Winnie The Pooh?", *the principal condescendingly retorted.*

"John Ambrose McClaren.", *Brylee cut in,* "We were watching 'To All The Boys: P.S. I Still Love You' last night, you'll have to excuse her, she picked a few things up.", *she attempted to save Quinn from end of the year detention.*

Mrs. Shay shot Quinn a look that read, "You're safe this time, don't forget who's in charge of graduation.".

"As fun as this little get together was, I need to get to class; I take my final 2 tests today, then I'm out of here.", *Quinn leaned over to whisper something in Brylee's ear,* "And this is one of those things that doesn't deserve my attention.".

Brylee accidentally let a little chuckle out, and Quinn threw up her signature peace sign, then walked off in the other direction. Mrs. Shay stood there staring at Bry with cold eyes, and a lukewarm smile. It was unsettling, she seemed to be having an off-day.

"Are you okay, Mrs. Shay?", *Brylee asked.*

"Of course! Why wouldn't I be?".

"I don't know, you seem… off.".

"How so?", *she replied with attitude.*

"I don't know. I didn't mean to offend you, I just wanted to check in and make sure everything is alright.".

"Hm. Perhaps you're just feeling a little biased this morning, with the switch and all, I can see how that might affect our dynamic.", *Shay left just as quickly as that jab left her mouth.*

'What switch? What is everyone talking about?", Bry thought to herself, confused.

Just then, Mrs. Shay sharply turned around.

"Oh, by the way, that Dianne from the police station, she's here for an assembly today, 10 o'clock on the dot, try not to be late.".

Brylee carefully nodded, with defense in her eyes.

"Why is she acting so different.. so suddenly? I've never seen her like this. It has to be about Jason, the timing is too weird, too 'coincidental'.".

As she stood there in her own little world, pondering, she was brought back to reality by the sound of heavy footsteps behind her. Curious, she turned around to see Jason walking entirely too close to her. Her insides wanted to freeze up, but she fought it, and allowed her outside to remain confident.

"Is he coming to confront me? Does he know yet? Why isn't he in class? What are the chances that him and I are alone in the hall together?! Did he plan this? Will he say anything to me? Is it illegal for him to look at me.. or talk to me?", her thoughts were racing.

Yet again, she found herself zoned out, only paying attention to the thoughts competing for first place in her mind. Suddenly, she was jolted against her locker, almost falling, and her books were scattered across the floor. Disoriented, she heard something so familiar.

"Better be more careful Bry, wouldn't wanna dirty up your squeaky clean record; you should be more careful.", *those words fell out of Jason's mouth so smoothly, but the scrape they left felt like it came from the sharpest knife. His tone was ever so slightly threatening, obviously torturous.*

He had shyly bumped against Brylee in the hall, knowing what would happen; it was purposeful, the security cameras would pass it off as an honest mistake. While she was still processing what had happened, the bell rang, and students began flooding the halls like schools of fish; all the while, Bry kept her original position. When Q made her way back to the lockers and found Brylee in the same position she left her in (more or less), she became suspicious, and mildly concerned.

"Did you ever get to class?", *Quinn caught her attention.*

"Uh, no.. I actually finished my quizzes online, and I tested out last week; that's why my last class took so long.".

"Then why'd you even come to school today?".

"I came to finish the last few prom details, which I actually need to talk to Mrs. Shay about, for the assembly because by law I have to attend that, and to see if I could score any end-of-year extra credit.".

"The only person I know who tries to find more school to do, after finishing!", *Quinn said laughing and shaking her head,* "So, you didn't talk to Shay about prom already? Why'd she come over if you didn't talk about prom? She looked determined.".

"Yeah, I actually don't know. She seemed off. She reminded me about the assembly though, and told me that Dianne was here, so, maybe that's why.", *Brylee responded.*

"The lady from the police station?".

"Yeah.".

"Maybe Shay is so 'off' because she's nervous about that cop being here. Maybe she's hiding something, you know, she has quite the ability to remain —

"Sneakily silent. I know. Thank you, walking conspiracy.", *Bry shot her a smirk and a look that read, "you're crazy".*

"The game is afoot.", *Quinn puffed up and smiled.*

"Sherlock?".

"Enola.".

"Of course.".

"So, you're ready to leave then? I finished my tests, I'm ready to go.", *Quinn asked.*

"Uhm.. almost.".

"Almost? Still chasing extra credit?", *Quinn poked.*

Back to School   97

"No, actually. I'm not gonna ask about that, but, remember, I have to stay for assembly, and I really should talk to Mrs. Shay about prom.".

"Okay, I'll stay for support.".

"And because I'm your ride?".

"Yes, but mostly support.", *Q jokingly squinted at Bry,* "It's at 10, right?".

"Yes.".

"Well, that's in 25 minutes, can you talk to Shay now, and still make it to the assembly on time?".

"I'm gonna try. What are you gonna do in the meantime?".

"I'll just sit outside the office.".

"Alright, let's go.".

The girls quickly started toward the principal's office, hoping to complete their tasks in one fell swoop.

Chapter 11

THE ASSEMBLY, THE TRUTH, THE SWITCH

The girls made it to Mrs. Shay's office with 20 minutes to assembly, Quinn took a seat outside, Brylee earnestly headed in. The minute she entered, she noticed a familiar face next to Shay; meanwhile, outside, a familiar face took a seat next to Quinn.

"Leo?", *Quinn excitedly asked, a bit shocked.*

"Hey, Quinn!", *he replied with a smile, then leaned over to give her a side hug.*

"I feel like I haven't seen you in forever!", *Q exclaimed.*

"I feel like I haven't seen you this excited before!", *he teased,* "We see each other around school all the time, girl.".

"Yeah, but I mean REALLY see, and talk.".

"Bruh, we were lab partners all year, we did nothing BUT talk.", *he retorted with sass.*

"Okay, fine. I haven't really talked to you in a couple of weeks.".

"Fair, I was busy, trying to grab some extra credit.".

"You sound just like Brylee, you two would be perfect for each other.", *Quinn chuckled, and rolled her eyes sarcastically.*

"Speaking of... how is she?", *Leo asked, clearly interested.*

"Brylee?", *she replied with a cheeky grin.*

"No, the frog we dissected a couple months ago.. yes, Brylee!", *he chuckled, shaking his head.*

"She's a little stressed, but good, all things considered.", *Quinn spilled without thinking.*

"All things considered? I'm sensing piping hot tea?", *he playfully inquired.*

"Tea, indeed; but, I can't tell you; at least until the kettle has cooled.".

"Got it, totally respect that. Is there any way I can help?".

"Maybe just, keep an eye out for Bry, if anything seems out of the ordinary, text this number.", *Quinn handed him Dianne's card.*

"Who's Dianne?".

"Let's just say, she's the ice to B's tea, for now, at least.".

"Alright, happy to help.", *he replied determined.*

"Thanks. I appreciate you, Leo.", *Quinn warmly thanked him.*

"No problem. Okay, girly, I gotta get out of here; apparently today's assembly is mandatory, I wanna get the good part of the floor, closest to the door, furthest from the smell of old turkey and mayonnaise packets.", *Leo announced,* "Save you two a seat?".

"Sure.".

"Shall I leave a seat for Reese?", *Leo tested, knowing that he would get a reaction.*

"How did you—

"It's really not hard to tell.", *he chuckled as he stood up.*

"Go get your non-turkey/mayonnaise seat, nerd.", *Quinn rolled her eyes as she smiled, thinking about Reese.*

"Mmhm. See you at ten.", *Leo began walking away.*

"Leo!", *Quinn shouted, hoping to catch his attention before he left.*

Leo stopped, turned around, and looked at her with his eyebrow raised.

"Have you ever tried, you know, talking to Brylee? Telling her how you feel?", *Quinn challenged.*

"I left her a note a little while ago.. so far, she hasn't responded.", *he replied while twirling around and walking the other way,* "But, when at first you don't succeed, try, try again!", *he exclaimed as he turned the corner.*

Quinn smirked, satisfied with the new information, and texted Brylee.

To: B

"Almost done in there? They're on in 12 minutes.".

9:48 a.m.

Bry glanced at her phone, but ignored the message. While Quinn was catching up with her lab partner/ unofficial second best friend, she was being force fed a hard to swallow pill.

"What do you mean, there's been a switch?", *Brylee impatiently asked.*

"I mean, you're no longer in charge of prom. I thought that was pretty clear.", *Mrs. Shay nonchalantly replied.*

"You can't just do that, I've already—

"Actually, Ms. Brylee, I am the principal, so yes, I can do this. Not to mention the immature ruckus you've started with Jason; you know he's—

"You could hardly refer to the harassment of this young girl as immature ruckus.", *Dianne cut in.*

"Well, she's the principal, so, she probably can.", *Bry quipped, cocking her head, and shifting her squinted gaze at Shay.*

"That's pretty bold attitude, considering I'm in charge of who graduates and who doesn't.", *Mrs. Shay threatened.*

"That's a pretty stupid threat, considering there's a police woman in this very room with you.", *Mrs. D said with attitude, as she whipped her body around in such a way that said, "The audacity!".*

"Right. Anyways, Ms. Brown, Ms. Walker has agreed to fill your space. You're off the prom committee; now, if you'll excuse me, I'm the opening act for this so-called 'mandatory' assembly.", *Shay remarked, cold as ice.*

Mrs. Shay swiftly left the room, and Dianne didn't take her eyes off of her until she turned the corner down the hall; once she was out of sight, Mrs. D compassionately looked at Brylee, who was still in shock.

"I don't trust that woman. Is she always like that?", *Dianne questioned.*

"Never. She's usually as bubbly as I am, I've never seen her like this, and she's been my principal for 4 years! I've always been her favorite student, she said so herself. She wanted to keep in touch even after I graduate! It's like she just flipped a switch.", *Brylee admitted, slightly hurt.*

"Right, well, I'm gonna look into her, Honey. Somethin' ain't right, I can feel it.".

"You don't think she had anything to do with this?", *Bry nervously asked.*

"I don't know, but, someone who truly cares for you wouldn't treat you like this after hearing that you've undergone a trauma. Not all that glitters is gold baby, some of it is just scrap metal catching the moonlight.".

"Well, some of that is J.R.R. Tolkien—

"And the rest is Mrs. D, Sugar!", *she warmly exclaimed, trying to make Brylee smile,* "You a Lord of The Rings fan?".

"Quinn is.", *Bry responded with a genuine smile.*

"There's the real Miss Brylee! I love your precious smile! Now, come on, Mrs. D will walk with you and Quinn to assembly.".

"What time is it?".

"Seven past, we better get down there.".

"*Sigh* Mrs. Shay told me not to be late.".

"All you missed was her 'opening act', and I think you got enough of that in here, at least it looked like the circus to me!", *Dianne opened the office door and motioned for Brylee to exit.*

Bry smirked as she walked into the hallway, and Mrs. D winked at her in a way that made her feel ever so slightly more comfortable in her current situation. Immediately, Quinn jumped up and started questioning her bestie.

"Hey! How'd it go? Shay looked pretty peeved, did you go over budget or something?", *Quinn chimed.*

"I'll tell you on the way home, promise.", *Bry assured her.*

"Okay, for sure. Everything okay, though?".

"Yeah, of course.".

"Hi, Sugar! You must be Quinn, I've heard so much about you!", *Dianne started.*

"Wow, no one's ever said that excitedly before.", *Quinn joked as they made their way towards the multipurpose room,* "You must be Mrs. D, thanks for taking such good care of my girl here.".

The Assembly, The Truth, The Switch

"Call me Dianne, Honey; and, I could say the same to you!".

"Okay, guys, it's time.", *Brylee pointed out as they made their way into the assembly.*

Quinn stopped Bry in her tracks, put her hands on her shoulders, looked her in the eye, and hyped her up; like those people do for boxers mid fight.

"You've got this! It's 20 minutes, in and out.", *Q said firmly.*

"Twenty minutes, in and out.", *Brylee repeated confidently.*

"Alright, girls, I'm going up and around on the other side of the stage; I'll meet with you afterwards.", Dianne informed them.

The girls nodded in unison, and began walking into the crowd.

"Where do we sit?", *Brylee asked.*

"I have seats reserved.".

"Okay, as long as it's not by the lunch window.".

"Why?", *Quinn looked at her, waiting to hear what she heard earlier.*

"It smells.", *Brylee shrugged.*

"Like what?", *Q pressed.*

"I don't know, old turkey sandwiches or something. Definitely some sort of expired lunch meat.", *she answered with widened eyes, and a faint look of disgust on her face.*

"Yeah, *chuckle*, I have the perfect seats; and there's someone I want you to meet, officially.".

Brylee looked at Quinn, a little sussed out, but, continued following her lead.

Chapter 12

ASSEMBLY II

Mrs. D started speaking just moments after the girls found their seats, Leo excitedly waved them over to where he was. Once they reached him, Q quickly introduced them to one another, and forced Brylee to sit in-between them.

"I'd love to talk more after the assembly, if that's alright with you, Brylee.", *Leo proposed.*

"Sounds great!", *Bry whispered,* "Let me give you my number.", *she motioned for his phone.*

"Definitely! Here.", *he handed it to her, under the radar, trying not to draw attention to them.*

"There ya go!", *Bry smiled, and quietly exclaimed, handing him his phone.*

"Thanks!".

Brylee's phone buzzed.

+1-553-258-0908

"Talk to you soon, M'ilady! - Leo Christianson".

10:15 a.m.

She looked at him and smirked.

"And, there you go!", *he whispered with a playful smile.*

"Thanks.", *she blushed, and looked toward the stage.*

Quinn was on the other side of Bry, trying to conceal her excitement; so far, her plan was working perfectly. On another note, all while Brylee's fairytale was just beginning, so was Jason's nightmare. He was sitting in the corner of the room, smug and disinterested; you'd think he'd be showing signs of contempt, or fear, but no. He was pretty unbothered for someone who was just served with a restraining order, and made to sit through an assembly that reminds him of that.

"Alright, girls and boys, ladies and gentlemen, men and women; today, I'm here to give y'all a warning. We're gonna be talking about things like boundaries, safety, respect, common sense, self defense, and protocol.", *Dianne was determined to keep the crowd engaged,* "Is everyone with me so far?".

"Yesss.", *the crowd replied in unison, with a lifeless tone.*

"I don't know if I heard y'all right, is everybody following me so far?", *Dianne asked again in a slightly louder, more sassy tone.*

"Yes, Mrs. D!", *the students replied, this time perkier and clearer.*

"Good. That's what I like to hear!", *Mrs. D continued,* "I'm happy to report that we don't have to do this kind of thing often, friends, but, something unsettling has happened at this school. Now, I won't name names, but, I will, however, tell you what happened.".

Just then, Principal Shay jumped from her seat, on the side of the stage, and interrupted Dianne.

"Sorry, students.", *Mrs. Shay said into the microphone,* "I need to speak to Mrs. D privately for a moment.

Dianne looked shocked, as Shay pulled her off to the side.

"You really do have nerve, don't you?", *Dianne said, slightly annoyed, while shaking her head.*

"This is MY school, and you cannot talk about what happened in front of all these students… its private. Confidential!", *Shay was heated, and had a look of fear painted across her face.*

"So, why do I have the feeling, you're trying to cover something up to save your own behind? How exactly are you linked to this incident, Mrs. Shay?", *Dianne quizzed her.*

The principal was trying to act unbothered, but she had too many obvious tells.

"I'm only trying to save the 'behind' of this school!".

"Mmhm. Well, in reply to what you barked at me earlier, only the names are confidential, the case is public knowledge. These kids, especially the girls, deserve to know what's happened here. Now, if you'll excuse me, I have some children to protect.", *Dianne began walking back to the mic,* "Oh, by the way, Mrs. Shay, if you want to appear innocent, don't try so hard. The more desperate to hide, the quicker you'll be found.".

Shay stayed where she was, shocked and outraged, she didn't move until Mrs. D finished her assembly, and she had to close it out.

"Students, let me get a round of applause for Mrs. D!", *Shay nervously commanded,* "I can confidently say, we learned so much today; not just as students and teachers, but as a family. Graduation is coming around so quickly, soon you will have left the nest, and you'll have to be watching after your own feathers; this was the perfect way to prepare you! Grades 9-11, please proceed to your next class, grade 12, have a wonderful rest of your week.", *she quickly descended from the stage, and made her way back to her office, but, before she could get out the door, Dianne stopped her.*

"What a wonderful speech! I sincerely hope you meant it. I just wanted to formally warn you that I'll be looking into you and the dirty little secrets that live under your school.", *Mrs. D informed, then began to walk away,* "Oh!

One other thing, that thing you said about the birds.. that was cute; however, these kids don't only have themselves—

"Yeah, yeah, they have you, I get it.", *Shay interrupted.*

"No. They have Someone else, if they so choose. Someone permanent, Someone Who's promised to never leave them. Although, He's not a bird, but, I have referred to Him as The Lamb.", *she added.*

Principal Shay, stood there, slightly confused for a moment, then stormed off in a fit of anger. Meanwhile, Brylee, Quinn, and Leo all caught up with Dianne before she headed out.

"The assembly was great, Mrs. D— I mean— Dianne!", *Quinn exclaimed.*

"Thank you, Honey Biscuits, I thought it went well too!".

"It was very informative, ma'am, thank you for taking the time to speak to us, and for your service on the force!", *Leo cut in, extending his hand for a handshake.*

"Well aren't you the complete opposite of the boy I just talked about!", *Dianne smiled and shook his hand.*

"I'd like to think so!", *he replied with a nervous chuckle.*

"Do you know my Brylee here?", *Dianne quizzed.*

"Sorta, I'd like to get to know her better, though. Quinn was my lab partner, I met Bry a couple times briefly, and there was just something special about her.", *he glanced over at Brylee who was blushing and softly smiling,* "Sorry, I hope that wasn't too forward.".

"Not at all.", *Bry replied.*

Dianne and Quinn smiled at each-other, almost speaking to one another with their eyes.

"Well, Sugar, it was nice meeting you.", *Mrs. D went in for another handshake,* "What was your name again?".

"Leo. Leo Christianson, ma'am.", *he replied as he shook her hand once more.*

"Call me Dianne, Baby.".

Leo nodded with a soft smile.

"It was lovely officially meeting you, sweetheart! You stay close to Brylee, okay?", *Mrs. D hugged Quinn.*

"It was lovely meeting you too, and of course!". *Q smiled as she pulled away.*

"And, my Brylee.", *she endearingly cupped her face in her hands,* "You, my dear, I will be seeing very soon. Periodically before the court date, and of course, on the day of.", *Dianne pulled her in for a big hug.*

"Thanks, Dianne. Am I allowed to bring anyone with me to the hearing?".

"Oh, Yes! Obviously your parents will both be there, since you're a minor; and you can bring these two wonderful people with you as well!".

"Great! I was actually just asking about Quinn, I don't think Leo wants to attend the hearing.", *Bry chuckled and looked over at Leo.*

"Actually…", *he jumped in,* "If you're comfortable with it, I would love to go and support you! I kinda put 2 and 2 together, but, maybe you can fill me in on some of the missing details before then?".

"Yeah, I am comfortable with that, actually. We'll talk about it later.", *Brylee smiled.*

"Cool.".

Leo matched her smile, as did Quinn. Q looked like a little kid at a candy counter, awestruck and excited by all the possibilities. Mrs. D brushed her hand against Bry's shoulder, and motioned that she was leaving. They said their goodbyes one more time, then went their separate ways.

"Hey, my parents want to know how my first day was, after all that… stuff, especially with the assembly today, and—

"Hey, relax, I totally understand.", *Leo cut off her rambling in the kindest, most understanding tone.*

"You do?".

"Yes!", *he quietly chuckled,* "Go, your parents should see you first, we can talk whenever you're ready.".

"I have a feeling that's gonna be realllll soon.", *Quinn happily mumbled in a sing-song tone.*

"I hope so.", *Leo smiled.*

"It will be.", *Brylee replied with a smirk and a reassuring tone.*

Leo motioned for the girls to head out of the door before him, he looked at Brylee.

"After you, M'ilady!".

"Thank you, kind sir.", *she happily played along.*

"And after you, Ms. Quinn.".

"Thank you, Leo.", *she rolled her eyes and giggled.*

"Alright, girls, I'm this way.".

"We're, that way.".

"Let me walk you to your car then.", *he gleefully offered.*

"Oh, no, it's okay, really!", *Brylee exclaimed, not wanting to burden him.*

"I insist, it's really no trouble at all.".

"You won't talk him out of it, B, this one happens to be a COMPLETE gentleman.", *Quinn teased.*

"Alright.", *Bry giggled,* "Walk us to our car.".

"I'm honored to escort you—

"M'ilady?", *Quinn cut in.*

"How'd you know?", *he asked.*

"Lucky guess.", *the girls started laughing.*

"'M'ilady? Where have I heard that before?", *Bry wondered as she held onto Leo's arm.*

"Lady Quinn, do you need to take an arm?", *he offered.*

"I think I'll wait for Sir Reese's arm.".

"Ah, yes, excellent choice, exceptional really!".

The girls laughed along as Leo walked them to their car, once he safely got them there, he side hugged them, then leaned down and kissed Brylee's hand. She blushed, and said goodbye once more. He watched as they pulled out, to make sure they got out okay, then headed to his vehicle as if he was floating amongst the clouds.

Chapter 13

THE QUESTION

On the drive home, Brylee told Quinn all about her visit to the principal's office, her demotion, and the incident with Jason in the hallway. Quinn was shocked beyond measure, she couldn't understand how Jason could get away with that, or how Mrs. Shay could so suddenly turn on her favorite student. The minute they turned into their driveway, Q found the words to say.

"Maybe I should've said something to Jenny this morning, or, should I say, Ms. Walker!", *Quinn exclaimed as righteous anger seeped from her pores.*

"That would've only upset you. Jenny got what she wanted, no comment is gonna get her bothered at this point.", *Bry attempted to calm her friend down.*

"Yeah, well, I just wish there's something I could've done.".

"Not everything is in your control, but, there may be something we can do now.".

"Who do I need to confront?", *Quinn asked in an intimidating tone.*

"Quinn, no. Not everything deserves your attention, ESPECIALLY negative attention! Remember?".

"I may remember something like that.".

"Mmhm.".

"So, what can we do then?", *she replied inquisitively.*

"We'll have to work with Dianne.".

"Can we bring Leo in on this?", *Q asked nonchalantly.*

Brylee blushed, gave her side eye, and smirked, knowing exactly what her bestie was doing.

"Playing match maker, are we?".

"Are you two not the perfect pair?".

"How could I possibly know that yet?!", *Brylee chuckled.*

"YOU BOTH SMELL WEIRD THINGS, FIRST OF ALL! Second of all —

"Hold up. What do you mean we smell weird things??", *she looked at her confused.*

"He said the cafeteria turkey smell thing before you did… plus, he said it smelled like mayo packets.".

"MAYO PACKETS! YES!", *Bry shouted her realization with glee and relief,* "I knew there was another smell.".

Quinn just stared at her smugly, knowing that her point was already being proven.

"What?", *Brylee jokingly rolled her eyes and shifted her gaze to Q.*

"Well, if you want to ignore what just happened here, I'll go ahead and tell you about the 'secondly'.".

"Go right ahead.".

"Bet. You BOTH finished school early, yet you BOTH were still chasing extra credit!".

"Who won the chase?", *Brylee asked intensely.*

"What?".

"Who won the chase?!".

"What do you mean???", *Quinn asked confused.*

"You said, 'he was chasing extra credit.', did he catch it? Or did it get away?".

"Yeah, he scored some extra credit. Why?", *she asked, still confused.*

"Can you ask him how he did it?".

"Are you STILL trying to get extra credit from the people who are currently under the rule of the woman who suddenly despises you?!", *Q exclaimed.*

"Despise is a strong word.".

"And an accurate one.".

"To answer your question, no, I was just curious.".

"Mmhm. And you still don't see how you're perfect for each-other?", *Quinn stared at Bry.*

"You're gonna have to give me a little more to go on than two VERY universal qualities.".

"That's what you call universal? So what do you call two people unfit for each other? Galactical?", *she sarcastically replied.*

"'Galactical' is not a word.".

"Fine. You want more? You're both super sweet, kind, respectful, funny, unique... you're both so special. He's been really into you for a long time, he's a perfect gentleman, super cute.. exactly your type. Smart too, obviously.".

"Why did he never tell me how he felt?".

"Apparently he did.".

"When? I don't remember that interaction. Seems like someone professing their love to you would be pretty memorable.".

"He said he left you a note a little while ago, but you never responded.".

"How little of a while?".

"I don't know, like a week or so I think.".

"Mmm, the only note I've gotten is the one from Jason.".

"Apparently not.".

"So, then, pray tell, where is the note?".

"Let me see the one Jason gave you.".

"It's in evidence.".

Quinn gave Brylee a look that said, "C'mon now.".

"But, I'll send you the picture I took of it.".

"That's more like it.".

"Still living inside your Enola persona I see?", *Bry poked.*

"The game is afoot.".

"There, I sent it. Did you get it yet?".

"Yeah, it just came through.".

Just then, Bryan walked outside.

"KaraLee, Honey, they're home!", *he shouted to alert his wife.*

"Hey, Dad.".

"Oh child of mine, how long have you been home?".

"*Shrug*, a while, we left right after assembly.".

"You two didn't have plans?".

"We figured it was more important to come home and tell you guys about my day and let you know that I'm okay.".

KaraLee ran out and hugged both of the girls.

"How was your day, Sweet Pea?!", *her mom asked.*

"It was good, Mom.", *Brylee chuckled,* "Certainly not as bad as I thought it would be.".

"So everything is okay? Nothing we need to talk about?", *Bryan cut in.*

"My principal was a little weird today, but, that's about it— oh— and there was a minor incident with Jason, but I—

"No incident with that boy is minor, what happened? He isn't even supposed to be near you.", *Bryan quizzed.*

"I was alone in the hall and he purposely bumped into me so I'd drop my books, then told me to be careful, but, he made it look like an accident.".

"Did you tell anyone?!", *KaraLee worriedly asked.*

"I texted Mrs. D after assembly, she'll handle it.".

"Yeah, she called your mom and I after assembly, filled us in on everything she saw today.. including a new boy?", *her dad tested.*

Brylee got a little nervous, blushed, and tried holding back her smile.

"Oh, he's just her FUTURE HUSBAND!", *Quinn jumped in.*

"Quinn!", *Bry exclaimed.*

"What?! You know it's true! I see it in your eyes!!".

"I do too.", *KaraLee warmly added.*

"He's nothing like Jason, he's—

"Bry Bry, you don't need to frantically explain yourself, it's okay. Dianne told us what she saw, and what she felt, though I would still like to meet him for myself, he sounds like a good man. I'm happy about this, Sweetheart, I thought after this whole thing you'd be scared of boys. I mean, I do want grandchildren.", *her dad stopped her rant before it even started.*

"Bryan!", *KaraLee exclaimed.*

"Well not right this very second! But I do want them, you do too!".

They began laughing and shaking their heads at each other.

"When you talk about Jason, you say 'boy'; when you were talking about Leo, you said 'man'. Why?", *Brylee curiously inquired.*

"Nothing about Jason says 'man', especially after what he did, only a boy would act like that. But I heard how Leo carried himself today, and what really sealed the deal for me was, I heard that he wanted to come to the hearing with you. Only a good, young MAN would do something like that.", *he explained.*

Bry smiled, her heart was racing, her cheeks were getting redder and redder, she knew in her heart that Leo was right for her, and everyone she trusted and cared about was confirming it for her.

"Go hangout with Quinn, Honey.", *KaraLee commanded.*

"But, Mom, I need—

"To have fun. You've been under a lot of pressure lately. We know that you're okay, the last thing you need right now is to sit and rehash the Jason thing with us. Go, have fun, just be home no later than 11:30. P.M. of course.", *her mom smirked.*

"Thanks, mom.", *Brylee smiled and went in for a hug.*

"Yeah! Thanks, mom!", *Quinn exclaimed, and joined their hug.*

The girls started laughing, then waved Bryan over to join them. Bryan kissed all three of them on the head, pulled KaraLee closer into him, then motioned for the girls to go.

"Love you both!", *the girls shouted in unison, through the car window, as they drove into their next adventure.*

Chapter 14

THE HIDEOUT

The girls decided to start their adventure in a familiar place. They headed to their favorite hideaway, the more fairytale one. It was bright, but shaded, there were many, mossy, hanging vines that they had to duck; the ground was soft with bunches of clovers and wild grass, which were decorated with blue pansies and daises, and a few scattered, moss-covered tree stumps welcomed them to sit and stay a while.

The sun was warm, but the breeze was cool; and as they took their seats, they were splashed by little, hopping water-droplets from the nearby brook. The silence was almost louder than them, except for the occasional squirrel filling the air with his song of cracking acorns. As the girls settled into their home away from home, they continued their earlier conversation.

"So, why'd you wanna see the note anyway? What does it have to do with Leo's note?", *Brylee curiously asked.*

"Maybe nothing, but, Jason is super shady, obviously, so I just wanted to check it out.".

Quinn pulled up the picture, zoomed in, and began reading the note out loud. As she read, Brylee zoned out, she didn't want to hear Jason's sweet nothings, but, she didn't mind replaying her earlier encounter with Leo. Suddenly, she heard something so familiar, so sweet to her ears, but in a different context. As Leo said 'M'ilady' in her head, Quinn said it out loud.

"Did you just say, 'M'ilady'??", *Bry asked to make sure it wasn't all in her head.*

"Yeah, that's how he referred to you in the letter. How many guys call you that?".

"Just Leo.".

"Well, it looks to me like Jason did too.".

"Which is odd, because in person, Jason never called me that. Not even when he was at my house pretending to be my date. Never once did a 'M'ilady' come out of his mouth. Not even on text!", *she pointed out.*

"That is super weird.".

Quinn furthered her investigation by zooming closer and closer into the image until something caught her eye. She chuckled in disbelief.

"Why are you laughing?".

"We think it's weird that he called you, 'M'ilady', once and never again, homeboy can't even spell his own name!", *Quinn bursted into an uncontrollable laughter.*

"What do you mean? He spelled Jason correctly, J-A-S-O-N, Jason.".

"But, zoom in.".

"You're gonna have to help me out here, it still looks like Jason to me.".

"Okay, look…", *Quinn zoomed in further,* "The original writing was in cursive, but, he erased it and did print instead. If you look closely, he covered up a cursive 'L', with a printed 'J', so he accidentally spelled, 'Lason', not, 'Jason'.", *Q explained.*

"I guess that'a kinda weird, I've never accidentally written 'Drylee' instead of Brylee, on anything before.".

"Yeah, bro, same.", *Quinn agreed.*

Brylee's phone began buzzing.

From: Leo Christianson

"Hello, M'ilady! How'd it go with your parents?".

"Leo just texted me.".

"Yassss!", *Q exclaimed*, "Do you need help? Do you feel nervous?".

"No, actually, not this time.", *Brylee, pleased with the truth in that response, let out a soft smile.*

"I wonder if Leo will tour with us?", *Quinn teased.*

"Maybe.", *Bry replied confidently.*

Quinn, in shock of just how truly calm and confident her friend was right now, looked at her with wide eyes, and a jaw-dropped smile.

"What?", *B smirked at Quinn's response and peeked at her from over her phone.*

"Nothing, you're just different with him.".

"Good different?".

"Very good different.".

As Brylee texted away, Q laid back in the clover, and took stock of every beautiful detail above her; she closed her eyes, and was almost lulled to sleep by the sound of her own heartbeat, but before she could fully doze off, an incessant vibrating caught her attention. She grabbed her phone and saw 4 messages from 'Newb', and 1 message from Leo. She looked over at Brylee to see that she was still texting with a smile on her face, then opened up her messages.

From: Newb

"Hey, Q-Tip, what are you doing?".

"I miss your beautiful face.".

"And your pretty voice.".

"And your sass LoL.".

Quinn couldn't wipe the smile off her face, his compliments were pulling the corners of her mouth wider and wider.

To: Newb

"Hey, Newb, I'm chillin' with Brylee. Wbu? That's sweet <3 I miss you too, your handsome face, your voice, and YOUR sass LoL!".

Delivered

While she was awaiting his reply, she received another text from Leo. She temporarily switched text threads.

From: Leo

"Hey, Quinn. Do you know if Brylee has a prom date?".

"Never-mind, she just filled me in on Jason. Do you think she's open to going with someone else, or is she kind traumatized from that experience?".

Quinn's heart was dancing inside her body, excitement for her best friend was bursting forth from her.

To: Leo

"Hey, sorry about the late response. She's totally open, not traumatized at all. You gonna ask her?".

…

"I want to. Any advice?".

"Do it.".

"LoL, thanks.".

"No problem.".

Quinn's smile kept growing wider and wider; reasons to grin just kept piling up. As her imagination ran wild, planning the rest of her bestie's life, Reese texted her back.

From: Newb <3

Brylee peeked over and noticed the new edition to Reese's contact name.

"Wowww, someone earned a heart!", *Bry teased.*

"He sure did.", *Q gave her a cheesy smile.*

"You grew! You didn't even try to deny it, you are unashamed!", *she excitedly replied.*

"What can I say? I'm too busy falling completely in love with him, to be caught up in shame. That's what I was talking about, shame and brooding doesn't deserve my attention anymore; there's better things to focus on.".

Brylee looked at her best friend endearingly, and smiled.

"I'm so proud of you, Quinn.".

"I'm proud of you too, Bry.".

"So, how's Leo?".

"He's amazing. Apparently he has little hideouts too, he's at his right now, reading and texting me.", *a grin started making its way back onto Brylee's face.*

"I remember him mentioning a hideout a couple times during lab. He likes to study botany.".

"Yeah, he did mention that.".

"I see a lot of flowers in your future, B, prepare yourself.", *Quinn poked.*

"I've never been more ready.", *she replied as she began to daydream.*

"It's getting a little hot right here, do you mind if we go deeper in and find some more shade?", *Q asked.*

"You sure it's not just Reese getting you all hot and bothered?", *Bry chuckled.*

"Ew, don't say 'hot and bothered'.", *she chuckled back.*

"Alright.", *B controlled her laugh and urge to tease her friend,* "Let's go find some shade.".

The girls got up and began walking deeper into their fairytale land, they've never explored the whole woods before, but if the heat kept breaking through the trees so intensely, they were gonna have to go deeper than they ever have.

"Here?", *Brylee asked?*

"Mmm, not enough clover to sit on.".

"True.".

The further they walked, the more shade they found. They stumbled upon a beautiful new location to add to their list, it had a rainbow of flowers, a small waterfall, thousands of vines, thick trees, and unique rock formations.

"Woah.", *Quinn gasped.*

"Woah indeed.".

"Why have we never ventured out this far before? We always stay so close to the parking lot.".

"Probably so we don't get lost.".

"That's not funny, Quinn.".

"I know it's not.".

Bry looked at Q a bit concerned at her statement.

"Don't worry, we won't get lost!", *Q blurted.*

Brylee nodded, and continued exploring. She ran her hand under the icy waterfall, picked a few vibrant flowers, and sat on the cushiest clover she's ever felt. Q walked slightly in the opposite direction, exploring the rock formations, and seeing if the vines were strong enough to hold her.

"You're not Tarzan, you know.", *Bry playfully shouted.*

"Okay, Jane.", *Quinn quipped.*

Quinn grabbed a sturdy vine, jumped, and curled her legs under, hoping to float and sway from side to side. She got, maybe, 7 seconds on it before it snapped and she landed on a patch of flowers.

"QUINN!", *Bry exclaimed as she ran toward her,* "Are you okay?! I told you, you're NOT Tarzan!!!".

"Um, ow.", *Q giggled as she braced her tailbone.*

"Hey, what's that?".

A pencil and sketchpad hiding in the crook of a boulder caught Bry's attention.

"I'm just glad I didn't land on that.", *Quinn joked.*

"I wonder if someones looking for this.", *she grabbed the book and opened it to see if there was a return number.*

"Hey, there's a book too. "Flora's Kiss". Whoever was here sure likes romance.".

"Let me see it.".

Quinn handed it over, and Brylee started flipping through it.

"This isn't a romance, it's about flowers, and plants, and nature.", *she announced.*

She set the book down and started exploring the sketchbook, it was full of color. Flawlessly sketched flora covered in eye-catching oil pastels, all marked with a capital, cursive 'L'.

"Q.".

"Hmm?", *Quinn broke eye contact with her phone screen and looked at Brylee.*

"These are the most beautiful sketches I've ever seen. Look.", *Bry handed her the sketches.*

"Wow, these are beautiful, so much detail.", *she flipped through the pages,* "Huh, this 'L' looks familiar.", *Quinn handed back the book.*

"Familiar like how? Do you think a famous artist gets his inspiration here?".

"Maybe.", *she went back to texting Reese.*

Brylee kept flipping through the pages, each one more realistic than the last; these drawings made you feel something, it's like it drew out your most vulnerable feelings. They were truly special. As she was staring at a gold and pink poppy, the clovers behind her started shaking. She thought it was just the steady breeze picking up until she heard something familiar.

"Did you find what you were looking for?", *a handsome voice cut through the quiet.*

Chapter 15

FLOWERS

Brylee whipped around, and Quinn's jaw dropped; the familiar voice matched an even more familiar face. There Leo was, standing with flowers and wild berries in hand. Bry nervously jumped up, the way you would if you had just been caught going through someone's dresser drawers.

"I—uh. I was just looking to see if there was a phone number or return address inside, I thought someone lost this.".

As Bry quickly handed him his sketchbook, and took a step back, Quinn stayed cool as a cucumber, enjoying the plot twist at hand; all the while, Leo's countenance stayed calm and soft, complete with a little smile.

"Brylee..", *he cordially chuckled,* "It's okay, it's a sketchbook, not a secret; I'm not mad, you don't have to be nervous. Besides, I would never hide anything from you anyways.", *he said as he handed the sketchbook back to her.*

"What are you doing?", *Bry asked.*

"Letting you finish looking through it.".

"Hold up.", *Quinn interrupted,* "I've got a question. I thought you were at YOUR hideout.".

"I am at MY hideout.", *Leo laughed as he playfully replied,* "I suppose now it's more of OUR hideout.".

"Sir, this has been our hideout since we were kids, and we've never seen you here.", *Q retorted.*

"Mine too.", *he admitted,* "And, in truth, I've never seen you two here either; where do you usually hangout? In this spot?".

"Nooooo.", *Brylee sarcastically laughed,* "We stay more toward the entrance, closer to the parking lot, that way we don't get lost.".

"Well, that explains it; I always hangout in the deeper parts, I find more beauty there.", *he made eye contact with Brylee,* "Although, it's evident that there was an even more treasurable, undiscovered beauty in the shallow of the woods.", *implying that she was the beauty.*

Brylee blushed, and smiled at her feet; she was swoon. His voice was like the chocolate in a fresh pastry, dark, sweet, and gooey. He sent shivers down her spine with every glance, and gave her goosebumps at the very mention of his name. She'd never met anyone like him before, like the man that lived in the depths of her wild imagination; but here he is, making her most colorful dream come true. His words were like honey, coating her heart, his voice as strong as thunder, yet as gentle as a soft, English rain. His hands followed his voice, she felt safe. He was a true gentleman, respectful, and full of love; everything he said sounded like it came from a poem book or a romance movie, the man of her dreams.

They were only just graduating high school, but his gravitational pull, drew her in so fast and so intensely, yet so naturally. She wondered whether or not she was allowed to have such thoughts at her age, thoughts that far exceeded prom. Marriage, life, a family, destiny; truthfully, you're never too young or old to think about and crave your destiny. She saw herself spending the rest of her life with him, and somehow, she knew he saw the same.

"You're really talented, you know.", *Bry complimented him,* "I saw certain beauty in your sketches that I hadn't seen in these woods. An outstanding beauty, an eye-opening one.".

"Wow, thank you, Brylee. That means a lot coming from you, that's the deepest compliment I've ever gotten.".

"You're welcome, Leo.", *she softly smiled.*

"As much as I'm loving this moment right here, and believe me, I am…", *Quinn's smile was almost a foot wide,* "Reese wants to meet for dinner, you guys wanna come? I'm sure he won't mind.".

Leo looked at Quinn, then at Brylee, then back at Quinn.

"You sure he doesn't want you all to himself, Q?", *he checked.*

"Probably, I mean, who wouldn't; but, it'll be fine.".

Leo and Brylee laughed.

"Sounds good to me, what do you say? Wanna come?", *B looked at Leo.*

"Anywhere with you.", *he smiled.*

"Cool. Leo, I'm guessing you know the way out of here? I told Brylee I wouldn't get her lost, but, like you heard, we usually stay close to the parking lot.".

Bry shot her a look that screamed, "I knew you didn't know where you were going!". Q nervously chuckled, stood up, and handed Leo his other book and his pencil.

"Don't worry.", *he smiled and shook his head,* "I'll get you girls out of here.", *he shifted all his belongings to one hand, and motioned to hold Brylee's hand with his other. She excitedly grabbed his hand, and followed his lead.*

"Keep up, Quinn.", *Bry poked.*

"I'm comin', I'm comin'.".

Prom in the Rain

Chapter 16

SAY "I DO"

They made it out of the woods, Quinn took their car to meet Reese, Brylee decided to ride with Leo. He and Bry talked about everything that popped into their heads: art, school, their childhoods, their favorite things, their families, their dreams, their plans; there were no longer secrets between them, every intimate detail was now shared and cherished.

"I'm really glad we got this time to talk.", *he quickly glanced over and longingly smiled at her.*

"Me too.", *Brylee continued,* "Hopefully this doesn't sound weird, but, I feel like I've known you forever, to be honest.".

He smiled as he looked ahead at the road, and reached for her hand.

"I feel the same way, if it's weird, we'll be weird together.".

Brylee giggled.

"So, I know it feels like we literally already talked about everything under the sun—

"But, amazingly enough, you have more to say?", *Bry cut in, smiling.*

"Yeah!", *he laughed,* "But, it's more of a question.".

Suddenly, Brylee's phone started blaring.

"I'm so sorry! That's my school tone..".

"You don't need to apologize, go ahead and check it, it could be important, all things considered.".

"Thanks.".

Bry opened her email and saw a message from Mrs. Shay, her skin began to crawl as she read, SUBJECT: Valedictorian. She tried to steady her breathing before it picked up, but, it was pushing against her, trying to outrun her breathing exercise.

"Bry, are you okay?", *Leo asked, concerned, noticing the change in her breathing pattern.*

"The email is from Mrs. Shay, and it's titled, "valedictorian".", *Brylee confessed,* "And I told you how she's been acting.".

"Yeah… man, here, I'll pull over and we'll look at it together.".

Leo pulled off onto a little dirt section of the road, put the car in park, then looked at Brylee; her eyes were glued to her screen.

"Hey, look at me.", *he gently demanded.*

She looked up at him, and forced a small smile.

"You are amazing. You deserve to be valedictorian, if anyone has earned that title, it's you Brylee. You're smart, kind, innovative, driven, determined, not to mention breathtakingly gorgeous… no matter what that email says, don't forget that. Mrs. Shay doesn't hold your worth in her hands, and to be honest, the title of valedictorian doesn't define your worth either.".

She squeezed his hand tighter, and smiled.

"Thank you, Leo. You're so sweet.".

"Alright, M'ilady! Ready to open it up??", *Leo exclaimed, trying to get her excited.*

"Okay..", *she took a deep breath,* "I'm ready.".

Bry opened the email and began reading out loud.

"*Dear Ms. Brown, as I have stated before, you are our star student, or so I thought. I've come to find out that there's one student here who has far exceeded your grades and test times, and has made it through the year with close to no major incidents. As astonishing as those findings are, I assure you, they're true. I'm sorry to inform you that you will not be this year's valedictorian; nonetheless, good job on your academics, and congratulations on graduating. - best regards, Mrs. Shay.*", *Brylee's countenance darkened.*

"Are you okay?", *Leo asked.*

"Did you pick up on the fact that she said, 'no major incidents'?", *Bry looked at him with a fierceness in her eyes.*

"I did. I assume she was referring to Jason, which is messed up. What he did shouldn't effect your academic record, or your chance at valedictorian.".

"I think I'd feel better if the other student won purely because their academics were better.. it's the fact that she threw the Jason thing in my face.".

"I get that. Not to upset you, but, do you know who won?", *Leo inquired.*

"Yep, and she's probably receiving and deleting the opposite email from the VP right about now.".

While Leo and Brylee were getting back on the road, Quinn had already arrived at the restaurant, and was having a very new type of conversation with Reese.

"You're sure you don't mind them joining us?", *Quinn quizzed.*

"I promise.", *Reese reassured her with a smirk.*

"Cool, so, you said you wanted to talk about something?".

"Yeah, do you mind if we talk before we go in? It's a little loud in there.", *he requested.*

"Sure. I hope this is a happy conversation…", *Q playfully side eyed him.*

"I hope so too.", *he chuckled as he lead her to a more private corner of the property*, "I've been thinking about this everyday since I met you, and I feel like this is the right time to ask.".

Quinn's heart sped up as if it was trying to beat her in a race. Once Reese was satisfied with their location, he stopped, turned around, brushed Q's hair out of her face, and grabbed her hands.

"Since I first saw you, in class, I knew that I wanted to know you.", *he started*, "I wanted to know your heart, your soul, and every other detail that came with you. I wanted all of you, Quinn, every part I could get; and I still do.".

Butterflies flew a marathon through Quinn's stomach, her breathing picked up, and she felt happy tears forming in her eyes.

"Just watching you, I became interested, fascinated, intrigued..", *he continued*, "Getting to know you, as fast as it seems, I've grown to love you. To quote Justin Bieber..", he chuckled, "'They say you know when you know, well I know, I know you're the one.', and I know, Q-Tip. I want to get to know you more and more for the rest of my life, I want to fall in love with you over and over again every single moment that I take a breath. You're electric, and I know that if I don't catch your lightning, somebody else will.".

Reese got down on one knee and pulled out a ring box, as he slowly opened it, Quinn started crying. With her parents always gone, she had never felt chosen, or felt an intentional love from anyone but Brylee and her family; but, for the first time, here it was, right in front of her. He opened the box to reveal a custom ring, decorated with a metallic guitar pick, set with 3 emeralds.

"Reese, is that the pick I played with the first time we went out?", *she asked through a smile.*

"It sure is.", he returned a smile, "I knew you were my forever, so I wanted to save our first.".

He took the ring and slid it onto her ring finger, then stood up.

"Does it fit? Is it comfortable?", *he asked.*

"It's perfect.", *she squeezed his hand.*

"It's a promise, and hopefully an answer to my question.".

"And what's your question, Newb?", *she teased as she wiped her happy tears.*

"Will you go to prom with me, this Saturday, officially as my girlfriend?".

"What's the promise?", *she flirted.*

"That after prom, after graduation, after all of that… you won't be my girlfriend anymore.".

"What will I be?", *she asked concerned.*

"My wife.".

She softly gasped as her jaw dropped, then slowly pulled away.

"Does that mean no?", *he asked slightly disappointed.*

She looked at him, walked in close, and kissed him. When the kiss was over, he looked at her both pleased and surprised.

"That was my first kiss.", *Quinn admitted.*

"Thank you for letting me be a part of it.".

"I want you to be my last kiss too.".

"Was it that bad for you?", *he teased.*

"No, Newb!", *she playfully rolled her eyes at him,* "I'm saying yes to you. Yes to your question, yes to the promise, yes to forever with you.", *she stared into his eyes with a glowing smile.*

"I'm so glad this was a happy conversation.", *he poked.*

Reese picked her up, twirled her around in excitement, and kissed her again. As they walked to the entrance of the restaurant, holding hands, they heard a shout.

"Is that Quinn holding hands in public?!", *Brylee teased from the car window.*

"Indeed it is! What a sight to see, am I right?", *Quinn shouted back while laughing,* "We're gonna go inside and get a table, see you inside?".

"Okay, see you in a sec!", *Bry replied.*

Leo parked the car, came around to the other side, and let Bry out of the car.

"M'ilady.", *he extended his hand to help her out,* "Are you okay to go in?".

"Yeah, I'm good now. You know, you're right, there are more important things than valedictorian. Thank you for reminding me that my worth doesn't lie in the hands of my school.", *she grabbed his hand and got out of the car.*

"Of course, whatever I can do to help, Darling.", *he took her hand once more, and lead her into the restaurant.*

"Darling? That's new.", *she teased.*

"Do you like it?".

"I love it.".

"Good. I have a few other names still in my pocket.".

"Good.", *she copied his tone,* "You'll have to let me hear them soon.".

He smiled at her in amazement, then took her to the table where Quinn was excitedly waving them over.

"They're perfect for eachotherrrr.", *Q sang to Reese.*

"It looks like it.", *he replied with a slight chuckle in his tone.*

Leo and Brylee got settled into their seats and started studying the menu.

"So..", *Bry peeked over her menu, at Q,* "Have you checked your email in the last 30 minutes?".

Leo's ears perked up and he became curious.

"No, I was in the middle of something important, that we need to talk about later by the way.", *she giggled,* "Why? Did you email me?".

"No, but, school probably did.".

Immediately, Leo's eyes widened and his lips parted in surprise, it was in that moment, Brylee told him all he needed to know about the situation. It was evident who would be this year's valedictorian.

Chapter 17

FOREVER? YES, FOREVER.

"Why would school email me? Do you need me to check it right now?", *Quinn asked.*

"No, I'm positive that it can wait.", *Leo forced a chuckle and looked over at Brylee.*

"Hey, man, I don't think we've officially met, I've seen you around school before though, I'm Reese Spencer.", *he reached across the table to shake Leo's hand.*

"You're right, bruv, I don't think we've met.", *he shook his hand,* "Pleasure to meet you, Reese; I'm Leo Christianson!".

"Where's the accent from? Don't hear many of those around Friday Harbor.", *Reese quizzed.*

"England, actually, mate. But, I've lived here quite long enough to be considered a Washingtonian.", *he poked.*

"I don't even think we consider each other that.", *Brylee looked at him and giggled.*

The group spent their time together laughing, sharing stories, swapping phone numbers, and of course, eating. Leo was relieved that Brylee got distracted from the valedictorian subject. After, about, 2 hours, they got the check and headed out.

"Thanks for paying, Leo.", *Bry smiled.*

"Of course, Love, I'm happy to have been able to.", *he replied with a smile as he grabbed her hand.*

"I see you pulled another out of your pocket.", *Brylee whispered to him.*

"And there's plenty more where that came from, Love.", *he replied, also in a hushed tone.*

"I think that one's going to be one of my favorites.".

He playfully smiled at her and winked, as they approached the parking lot, Reese cut in.

"Thanks for paying, Man! I got the next one.".

"No problem, Bruv! Sounds great, looking forward to it. Text you later?", *Leo replied.*

"Yeah, bet.".

They dapped each other up, and the girls giggled at the sight of it.

"What are you two laughing at?", *Leo joined their laughter.*

"Oh, nothing, nothing.", *Quinn replied, holding back her laughter,* "But, uh, real quick, B, dap me up, dap me up.", *she teased and nodded as a guy would.*

"Betttt, bet.", *Bry followed.*

The girls dapped each other up the same way Leo and Reese did, but, with more laughter.

"Alrightt, alrightt.", *Reese smiled,* "Don't hate on the bros.", *he said, chuckling.*

"Oh, don't hate on the bros!", *Q teased him.*

He looked at her, smirked, grabbed her hand and pulled her close enough to put his arm around her shoulder.

"Well, then. She got real quiet real quick.", *Bry quipped.*

"Don't worry, it won't last long.", *Reese poked.*

Quinn playfully smacked his arm as she smiled and shook her head.

"So, what's the plan?", *Leo asked.*

"Well, me and Bry don't have to be home till like eleven.", *Quinn replied.*

"Eleven, huh?", *Reese got a certain look in his eye.*

"Yeah, why? What'd you have in mind?", *Brylee inquired.*

"I feel like we should all do something together, this is a fun little group.", *he responded.*

"I agree.", *Q nodded.*

"Are you up for it?", *Bry shifted her gaze to Leo.*

"Absolutely. Anywhere with you, anytime.", *he kissed her hand.*

Brylee blushed as they walked toward their cars.

"Girls riding with guys?", *Reese asked as he looked at the girls.*

"Yeah.", *they replied in unison.*

"So, what exactly are we doing?", *Leo questioned.*

"Yeah, wait.. we don't even—

Brylee was cut off by the sound of police sirens.

Forever? Yes, Forever.

"Sorry, that's Mrs. D, I better answer it.", *Brylee looked at Leo as she pressed answer,* "I promise my phone doesn't usually go off this much.".

He smiled at her and slightly chuckled.

"I believe you.".

She put the phone to her ear, everyone got quiet, and Quinn got closer to Bry so she could hear.

"Hey, Dianne!".

"Hi, Sugar! How are you?".

"Good! Hanging out with Quinn, Reese, and Leo.".

"Oooooo, Leo, huh?", *she teased.*

"Yes.", *Brylee giggled.*

"Well, I'm sorry to interrupt, but, I've dug up a few things on that Mrs. Shay, and I think you should come down to the station right now so we can talk about it. Your friends can come!".

"Okay, it's alright. I'll be right there, but, I'll just have one of them drop me off, they probably don't wanna c—"

"We'll be there!", *Quinn, Reese, and Leo shouted simultaneously.*

"Perfect, Sugar, see you soon. Bye!".

Mrs. D hung up the phone, and Brylee looked at her friends.

"So you could hear her then?", *she chuckled, with one eyebrow raised.*

Everyone nodded.

"Pretty much.", *Quinn replied.*

"Well, now we do have a plan! Let's go.", *Reese exclaimed.*

"Indeed we do!", *Leo added,* "Should we get going?".

"Yeah. See you guys there.", *Bry hugged Quinn and knuckle bumped Reese.*

"See you there.", *they replied as they got into their car.*

Everyone quickly made their way down to the station, it was only 10 minutes away from the restaurant. As they were driving, Brylee remembered something.

"Hey, didn't you want to ask me something before you got cut off by school?", *Brylee asked.*

Leo smiled as he pulled into the parking lot.

"I do, in fact, have something to ask you.. but, I want to do it in a place that holds happier memories. I can't imagine that this place is a hub of joy for you.".

"Yeahhhh.", *she giggled,* "Not exactly.".

"Thought so.".

He parked, and Reese pulled into the spot next to them. The men helped their ladies out of the cars, and they all headed to the front door. Before they entered, everyone stopped Brylee.

"You okay?", *Quinn checked.*

"I'm okay.", *Bry responded.*

"You sure?", *Reese and Leo quizzed.*

Bry chuckled and squeezed Leo's hand.

"Guys, I promise I'm good. The first time is the scariest, this should be fine.".

Forever? Yes, Forever.

They looked around at each other, almost for confirmation, nodded, then headed in. Right away, Mrs. D spotted the crew and happily motioned for them to meet her. They walked to her window, grabbed 2 extra chairs, then all took a seat.

"Hey, Babies!", *Dianne exclaimed,* "You been having a fun day?".

They all spoke on top of one another, saying "yes", in their own way.

"Good.", *she nodded in approval,* "Then, I'll try not to keep you too long.".

Dianne began pulling up records on her monitor, and spreading out papers, marked up in red ink, in front of Bry.

"I've been doing some research into this Shay character…", *D started.*

"Look, B..", *Quinn whispered,* "She started her investigation before you.", *she teased.*

Brylee jokingly rolled her eyes at her and put her focus back on Dianne.

"As you may have gathered from her title as "Mrs.", she's married; meaning, she has a maiden name. I decided to look into that angle, and I found something shocking; however, it may answer a lot of questions.", *she continued,* "Her maiden name is, brace yourself, Honey, McKinley.", *she paused, allowing Brylee to process that information, and pushed a paper toward her, confirming what she said.*

Bry's heart started racing, her palms got sweaty, and a million thoughts started piling up inside her head. There was a faint look of horror swept across her face.

"Sooo.. is she related to Jason?", *Quinn interjected.*

"That's what I asked myself. I supposed that McKinley could be one of the more common surnames, and it could be completely coincidental.", *Mrs. D replied.*

"So, was it, completely coincidental?", *Leo asked, eagerly awaiting an answer.*

"No, sir, it wasn't. They're pretty close, too, I took the liberty of sifting through her social medias, and this is what I found.", *Dianne handed her phone to the group.*

They all gathered around to look, and what they saw left them speechless, in complete and utter shock, flabbergasted. Reese was the first to speak.

"Soo.. Mrs. Shay, aka, Brylee's principal, is her attacker's aunt?", *he asked for clarification, to make sure he took in that information correctly.*

"Correct, Sugar. Shay is Jason's aunt.".

"So, what? Is she mad at me? Does she blame me for what Jason did?", *Brylee asked with righteous indignation dripping from her every word.*

"I asked myself that question too. I did some more research and found that Jason is evidently their top lacrosse player, I also learned from an anonymous source, that he has a big league contract hanging in the balance, it's dependent on how his senior year plays out.", *Dianne went on,* "Apparently, he had an episode at a game, in front of a recruiter, so, they know about his anger streak. This was somewhat of a redemptive season for him, if he has any incidents, his contract goes bye bye.".

"So, because Shay knows that her nephew's lacrosse career has been compromised, for good this time, she's trying to sabotage Brylee.. to.. I'm guessing, give her a taste of her own medicine?", *Leo inquired.*

"That's what it looks like.", *D replied.*

"Can she get away with this?", *Quinn asked.*

"Technically, if she's subtle enough and covers her tracks well, yes, because right now, the court would call this 'conspiracy', however, I'm gonna present it as motive for her misbehavior. If it gets out that Mrs. Shay is, indeed, willing to sabotage her own students, she will never work with children again. This is a classic case of nepotism and entitlement, and I won't let her get away with it; don't you worry, Sugar.", *D reassured them,* "Oh!—one more thing— I took a closer look at that note that Jason wrote you, I was trying to get a baseline for his behavior. I compared it to his text messages, and it didn't match up at all. I also had our writing analysis team compare the handwriting to that of some papers he wrote for school, totally different handwriting.", *she brought the note out,* "They also found traces of eraser shavings, which is common, but paired with the handwriting, and the fact that the only section of the paper to be touched by an eraser was the name portion.. I have reason to believe he took credit for someone else's letter.", *she handed the letter to Brylee.*

Leo glanced over at it as Bry was folding it up.

"Wait!", *he exclaimed,* "Can I see it for a second?".

"Sure.", *Bry shrugged and handed it to him.*

He quickly unfolded it, and his eyes widened.

"Is something wrong?", *Quinn asked.*

"This! I wrote this! I left this note for you, Brylee.", *Leo looked at her a bit shocked,* "I used this to try and confess my feelings to you.. when you didn't respond to me, I thought you might've been disinterested.".

Brylee's jaw dropped.

"Here.", *he handed the note back to her,* "This is the question I've been wanting to ask you.".

She gave him a soft smile.

"I know the setting isn't ideal.. but, the invitation stands. Will you come to prom with me, Love?".

A wider smile started growing on Bry's face.

"Yes! I would love to!!", *she jumped across her chair and hugged him,* "Finally, a happy memory here.", *she poked.*

As they were enjoying their moment, Quinn was as well; without thinking, she started shouting in excitement.

"Brooooo!!! You and Leo start going out on the SAME day I say 'forever' to Reese! This is like the most best friend thing we could—

"Wait..", *Brylee cut in*, "Did you say forever?".

Chapter 18

CONVERSATIONS

They finished up at the police station with more than enough time to hangout, but, since Quinn dropped that bomb, all Brylee wanted to do was go home and talk about it. They had all decided on going bowling, and were driving to the ally right now, separately, of course.

"Are you okay?", *Leo asked, slightly concerned.*

"Yeah. Nothing about this 'McKinley case' even surprises me anymore.", *she dryly replied.*

"That's not what I mean.".

"Then, what do you mean?", *she inquired.*

"I mean, ever since the email earlier, you've been slightly off.. I mean, I get it; but, I think it's seeping into other areas of your life, Love.".

"What do you mean?".

"Well, you didn't seem very happy for Quinn about her big news, that's not very on brand for you.".

"Yeah, well, I was upset that she didn't tell me sooner.".

"I think if she could have, she would have.".

"Why are you defending Quinn all of the sudden?!", *she copped an attitude, slightly raised her voice, and turned in her chair to face him.*

"I'm not trying to defend Quinn, I'm trying to make sure you aren't throwing away your friendship over an academic title that does nothing but fuel pride! I mean, it's a wonderful honor, and it's amazing that you were even considered, but, if it comes at the risk of your friendship, I think that it has turned to something ugly at that point. I think if you're not careful with your focus, it can turn into a breeding ground for pride, which pushes people away.", *he softly exclaimed, trying to communicate well.*

Brylee turned back in her chair, and faced the window. After a few minutes of silently watching the grass pass by, she began to speak.

"I'm sorry, Leo. I shouldn't have raised my voice, you were being so mature and calm and collected; thank you for that.", *she muttered in remorse.*

"Brylee, I forgive you. Something I want you to know about me is, I will never treat you like Jason did, I will never disrespect you, or raise my voice at you, or make you feel unsafe. I know you're under a lot of pressure right now, prom got taken from you, the court case, graduation, restraining orders, Quinn moving into a new phase of life, life outside of school is getting ready to begin; but, that pressure is not gonna crush you, it's gonna create something special, beautiful.. even more so than a diamond. We have choices, and I think you should choose not to surrender your lifelong friendship to those pressures.", *he reached for her hand,* "I'm here. I want to be next to you well after prom, well after graduation, well after you begin your career, well after you find out who you were meant to be. Brylee, I want to be with you every moment.".

Bry started tearing up, and took his hand.

"You don't have to worry with me, but, one thing you can count on is.. out of care for you, if I see you heading onto the train tracks, I'm gonna alert you and try to pull you out of the way when a train is speeding toward you.", *he stroked her hand with his thumb, attempting to comfort her.*

She looked at him, relieved, with a soft smile on her lips.

"I've never met anyone like you before.. except for Quinn, kinda.", *she chuckled.*

"I've never met anyone quite like you either, Darling; and I'm incredibly grateful to have been given the chance to know you.", *he smiled as he stopped at a red light.*

As they were stopped, a call came through on Leo's car.

INCOMING CALL FROM: THE BRO

Brylee looked at him with an eyebrow raised and a toothy smile that stretched from cheek to cheek. Leo blushed as he looked at her, and awkwardly chuckled.

"Reese, I presume?", *she teased.*

"You presumed correctly.", *he replied as he pressed answer.*

"Hey, man, what's goin' on?", *Leo greeted.*

"Hey, Bro, you guys almost here?", *he asked curiously.*

"Almost. Are you two already there??".

"Yeah! For like 10 minutes.".

"How'd you manage that?".

"Police escort from Dianne—ow!", *he exclaimed as a slapping sound was heard.*

"Hey, Q!", *Bry laughed, knowing the sound was her.*

"Hey, Gurll!", *she exclaimed.*

"No, actually though, Bro, I just took a back way and it turned out to be a shortcut.", *Reese admitted.*

"Oh, alright, I took Baker to Clemens, so, I should be there in about 3 minutes.", *Leo replied.*

"Bet. For future reference, if you cut through the parking lot of the old baseball field on Wilson, then hang a right, a left at the next stop sign, then another left at the light, you're there in half the time.", *Reese explained.*

"I'm not familiar with the old baseball field. Is it by the station?", *he asked as he began driving again.*

"Bro! You've never played there?!".

"I cant say I have.", *Leo confessed.*

"I gotta take you there dude! It's like a rite of passage!".

"I'm up for it!", *Leo chuckled at Reese's enthusiasm,* "I'm pulling in now— oh — I see you.".

He pulled in next to Reese and hung up the phone.

"You ready to do this, Lovely?", *he asked Bry, with a smile.*

"Yes, thanks to you.", *she smiled and looked into his green eyes.*

She watched him closely as he left the car to open her door, studying him, so she could take in his every detail as he had so obviously taken in hers. The way his golden, sandy hair glistened in the evening sun, they way the rays caught his emerald green eyes and projected rolling, Irish hills of romance onto everything he looked at. The way his jawline connected his neck to his ear, they way he walked so confidently, so freely; the way he reached for the car door with such respect and love, so she didn't have to lift a finger. The way his smile dazzled and lit up the room, the way his strong hand reached when he offered her his hand, and the way his gentle grip caressed it, making her feel seen, known, and safe. She looked inward, to discover the intensity of her bursting emotions, and outwardly to remind herself of his. This was it.. Quinn found her forever, and Brylee did too.

Chapter 19

FREE TIME

The group had a great time bowling, their hangout looked like a scene in a movie; Leo even made a way for the girls to be able to talk. After their 3rd game ended, he suggested that him and Reese get the girls some food and play a few games at the arcade, so while they were having their 'bro time', the girls talked about everything!

Brylee apologized for acting weird, and opened up to Quinn about it. After hearing it all, Q reminded her that she had no interest in being valedictorian, and agreed with what Leo had said to her. After that was squared away, Bry asked her for details about her little moment with Reese, by the time she finished her story, Brylee's mascara was running down her face, she couldn't stop the happy tears. It was such a special feeling to be able to witness her best friend growing and taking down the walls that her parents built around her; brick by brick, that self loathing and pain was being dismantled and destroyed, for good!

They finished their activities by 10:15, and at that point, they were ready to get home; they headed back to the restaurant to pick up the girl's car, then went their separate ways. Over the next 3 days, (having finished with school early), they were inseparable. Everyday, they all got together and took turns doing what the other thought was fun; their adventures ranged from the movies, to painting, local concerts, to skating, picnics, to dinners at home.

During that 3 days, Bryan and KaraLee met and fell in love with Leo, the way they sensed the good in Reese, they quickly sniffed out the good in Leo. They even gave him their blessing to be with their daughter. Reese also took that time as an opportunity to speak with them about what he told Quinn, he shared his hopes and plans with them, and was honest about his intentions. After some careful thought, they gave him their blessing too, they decided that young marriage suited Quinn, as well as it did Brylee.

KaraLee shared how she always pictured her girls married at 20, with grandkids by 25, and Bryan shared how he always imagined the girls waiting to notice boys till they were well into their 70's, but, getting to know them, changed his mind. They even planned a biweekly family dinner, including the guys, so they could continue to get to know them better and see how they interact with their daughter.. and their.. well, daughter.

Brylee talked to Leo about the tour that she wants to take with Quinn, and found out that he'd love to be apart of it.. like he says, "Anywhere with you, always.". He didn't plan to go to college, so, it didn't really disrupt his plans. After a conversation amongst all 4 of them, they decided to run it by Bryan and KaraLee; they didn't say no, but, they said they would give them an answer after graduation. Since that moment, Quinn and Reese have been in contact once again with Mr. Walker.

So, now, here they are; it's Friday, prom is tomorrow, and they're ecstatic. Their suits are picked out and match the girl's dresses, all the details are handled, and they're celebrating with a baseball game at the park on Wilson.

"So, you've never been here before? Ever?", *Reese asked Leo, still a little shocked.*

"Never.", *Leo chuckled.*

"Do you even have baseball in England or is there just cricket?", *he asked, genuinely curious.*

Quinn looked at him like, "What are you even asking", which made Brylee laugh, and he shrugged like, "What?! It's just a question!".

"No, it's quite alright, Quinn.", *Leo started laughing,* "It's only natural to be curious about a place you're unfamiliar with. However, yes, I do know a thing or two about baseball, though, cricket—to be fair— IS widely played in England.".

"Cool! So, you know all the rules and things like that?", *he replied.*

"More or less, if there's something I'm not understanding, I'm sure you could help me out.", *Leo smiled, then looked at the girls,* "By the looks on your faces, I gather that you know how to play this.. and you know how to play it well?", *he asked, slightly intimidated by their game faces.*

"It's like Reese said the other day..", *Brylee shrugged and scrunched her mouth up and to the left,* "Rite of passage in this town.".

"I see.", *he smirked, intrigued by this new dimension of her personality,* "Well, then, let the game begin!'.

They rallied together and started their game, Reese, Brylee, and Quinn quickly found out that Leo excelled at baseball; evidently, when he was younger, he wanted to be a major league player, so, needless to say.. he trained A LOT. At first, Reese struggled to keep up with him, but, with a little determination, he matched his energy. The girls were shook, but, much like Reese, determined. They suggested a little girls against boys game.

"But, there's only 4 of us.", *Reese pointed out.*

"And?", *Quinn smirked,* "Sounds like more than enough to me.".

The guys accepted the challenge, and started a new game; they quickly got called out for not playing to their full potential, and were accused of just letting the girls win. Reese and Leo agreed, with their eyes, that it was time for full power; the game dragged on and had many nail-biting moments, but, ultimately, ended in a tie. Was it a genuine tie, or one orchestrated by the guys? I don't know, but, they didn't care. It wasn't about who won or lost, it wasn't about the men or the women, it was about laughter, and love.. bonding and true friendship. It was the perfect rite of passage for all of them, as a whole, stepping into a new time. Those games at Wilson field became a core memory, and, they would soon visit that feeling quite often.

The afternoon almost ended perfectly, but, what's a story without a little conflict? As they were wrapping up cleanup, the red dust started swirling in the air; Reese turned around to see someone walking onto the field with their equipment. He nudged Leo to look with him, and what he saw started a fire in his bones, however, he remained calm so he didn't upset the girls.

"Alright, ladies, we should get going. Where do you want to eat? Reese is buying.", *he took control.*

"Ummm.. burgers?", *Brylee suggested.*

"Eh. Pizza?", *Quinn countered.*

"Eh. Tacos?!"?

"Definitely not. I want fries, I know that.".

"Poutine?", *Bry suggested.*

"Bingo!", *Quinn exclaimed,* "There's that new place on Haven Ave., right?".

"Yes! Next to our Thai place.".

"OOOOOO, Thai!".

As the girls continued chattering amongst themselves, the boys grabbed all the equipment, and lead them forward towards the parking lot. Before they reached the end of the field, they heard a cold, sarcastic voice.

"What? I can't join the game?", *Jason nonchalantly shouted, in hopes he would get under their skin.*

Brylee, angry at feeling violated, stopped in her tracks, turned around, and made eye contact with him. Leo stood slightly in front of her, to act as a protective barrier. Quinn, being Quinn, took a baseball bat from Reese and started toward Jason; but, before she could get more than 2 feet out, Reese pulled her back.

"I like your energy, but, let's save it for something that doesn't get you arrested.", *Reese whispered to her.*

"Let's just go, Love, Let's leave him here and go get some food; he's only trying to irritate you.", *Leo said, looking into Bry's eyes.*

"You're right, but, first, I have something to say.", *she replied with a terrifying calm in her voice.*

She looked back at Jason.

"I'm not afraid of you.", *she raised her voice so he could hear her, and spoke with authority,* "Let me make this perfectly clear, you are to stop following me around, consider this your formal warning; since apparently the restraining order wasn't formal enough. Dianne will be hearing about this, I've already alerted her that you are WELL within 50 feet of me. I know you and your 'Auntie Shay's' game, and neither of you will get away with it. If you come near me again, I will defend myself. Do I make myself clear?".

"Crystal.", *he smugly retorted.*

Leo got a bad feeling that was followed by a rush of adrenaline.

"Girls..", *he spoke quietly and carefully as Jason walked closer to them,* "Go get in the car, NOW.".

They heeded his warning and headed for the car, as Bry walked away, Jason ran for her.

"Girls, run!", *Reese shouted,* "Get in and lock the doors.", *he firmly demanded.*

Reese and Leo pushed against Jason and held him off; Jason just kept trying to mow through them, almost knocking Leo down. Reese pushed him off, and he just stood there with a satisfied smile.

"What are you smiling about?", *Leo firmly asked Jason.*

"I don't think your girlfriend's little speech stuck. She didn't even believe her own words. Tsk, tsk, tsk, no wonder she isn't valedictorian.", *he threw knives with his tongue.*

Reese looked at Leo, wondering if he was gonna have to hold him back, but, all Leo did was take a deep breath and a step toward Jason.

"I can assure you, she meant every last word, Jason.", *he calmly, and quietly said as he leaned closer to his ear.*

The way it happened both intimidated Jason, and fueled his fire. After he said that to Jason, they walked to the car, watching their backs, as Jason just stood staring. They got in the car and made sure the girls were okay.

"Okay, executive decision, we're grabbing fast food and heading to the station; you need to file a report, right now.", *Leo said as he looked into Brylee's eyes through the rearview mirror.".*

Bry nodded.

"Okay, good.", *he replied as Reese backed out of the spot.*

"I'll text mom and dad.", *Quinn assured B.*

"I'll get us to Dianne.", *Reese added.*

Chapter 20

SECRET SERVICE

Reese got them to the police station as fast as possible, and Dianne helped Bry file a report; she added her notes to the court case and assigned two patrol cars to follow Brylee and her friends around until after the hearing. Wherever they are, so are the officers. Until Monday, they had their own, personal secret service team. Bryan met everyone at the station to make sure they were safe, while KaraLee stayed home and made some comfort food.

"Are you sure you guys don't want me to drive you? KaraLee and I can come pick up your car later.", *Bryan pressed.*

"I'm sure, Dad.", *Brylee replied.*

"Sir, if you feel like you need to drive your daughters home, I completely respect that; Reese and I can just meet you guys there. Right?", *Leo looked over at Reese.*

"Absolutely!", *he quickly replied.*

"No, that's alright; I think it's pretty clear that my daughters feel and are safe with you two. You handled it well, thank you, Leo, and Reese, for protecting my girls.", *Bryan continued,* "I'm gonna get home and see if Kara needs any help, see you in a few minutes?".

"Yes, sir; we'll get them home now.", *Leo assured him.*

Bryan nodded, then hugged all 4 of them before walking out the door, as he was walking, they heard him talking to himself.

"I wonder who I have to talk to about getting my own security team.. I think I'm worthy of secret service.", *he mumbled to himself.*

The 4 of them snickered at Bryan's ability to lighten a heavy situation, while waving goodbye to Mrs. D. Once they got outside, Reese took one side of the car and Leo took the other, they were acting like the girl's personal secret service as well.

"I think we're safe.", *Quinn chuckled as she got into her seat.*

"And I fully intend to keep you that way, ma'am, ktchh (he made a radio noise as he spoke into his shoulder) over, breaker breaker, one-niner, bag secured, we've got two very safe, and very feisty ladies, over, ktchh.", *Reese pretended to be an officer.*

Leo heard him and immediately joined in, he too started talking into his shoulder as he got into the driver's seat.

"Ktchh, copy that, Spencer, bag is indeed secured, I can confirm I have one of the two feisty ladies locked in and secure, over and out, ktchh.", *Leo played along in an American accent.*

"I think these officers are my favorite.", *Bry giggled and looked at Quinn.*

The men smiled, happy with their performance.

"Oh definitely!", *Quinn started*, "Certainly less intimidating, so, that's nice.", *she teased as she looked into the rearview mirror.*

Leo got them home, and as they exited the vehicle, they noticed the two patrol cars parking across from the driveway.

"I guess secret service isn't that secret.", *Quinn quipped.*

"It's just something we'll have to get used to; it's only until Monday.. hopefully.", *Bry replied, trying to stay positive.*

They headed inside, and as soon as they stepped through the door, the smell of fresh herbs wafted their way, catching them up, and carrying them to the kitchen. KaraLee baked fresh bread, made homemade tomato soup with fresh herbs from her gardening project, gourmet grilled cheese, and rosemary, lemon, and thyme grilled chicken. It had been Brylee's favorite since she was a little girl, it always cheered her up; the tradition started when she broke her leg, it carried through skinned knees, and bullies, and here it is again, warming her heart.

"I smell 'feel better' food!", *Quinn exclaimed in a sing-song tone.*

"Your nose is correct!", *KaraLee matched her tone as she set the plates on the bar counter,* "Sit, sit, you guys have had a hard day.", *she insisted.*

Before Bry took her seat, she gave her mom a much needed hug.

"My Baby! Are you okay? I'm so sorry about what happened.", *her mom spoke gently as she caressed her face and examined her.*

Brylee offered her a soft smile.

"I'm okay, mama, it's okay.".

She stared at Bry for a few moments longer, just taking in her daughter's sweet face, then, gently nudged her to go eat. Kara walked over to Bryan and kissed him.

"What happened?", *she asked with widened eyes.*

"Well, I'll give you the little details later, but you have the gist of it. Also, there's two patrol cars outside—

"What?!", *she raised her voice in surprise, the kids pretended like they didn't hear her.*

"Shhh!", *Bryan shushed her,* "They'll follow all 4 of them around till after the hearing. So, when they're here, the officers are here; it's okay, Honey.".

"Okay.", *she composed herself and put on a smile as she walked back towards the kids.*

"Anybody want more?", *she asked in a peppy tone.*

Chapter 21

PROM, AND MAYBE MORE

It's finally here, prom. We've been waiting for this for forever, or at least, I have. Amazingly enough, Quinn isn't gagging at the mention of slow dances and photo booths, anymore; I knew if she had a date, she'd feel different about it. The day is stretching sooo longggg. My body woke me up early, and I woke Quinn up early, who accidentally woke my parents up early, we can't get ready too early, or our hair and makeup won't be fresh; if we start an activity, I think the hours might begin to fly by and we wont have enough time to get ready!

Honestly, I just need to find a way to calm down. There are a few things that aren't going according to my original plan though.. like..I never imagined I'd show up to prom with a police escort, but, we'll make the best of it! I also don't know how prom works with Jason there and a principal chaperone that despises you.. but, tonight isn't about them and their drama.

Quinn is excited too, however, she's much more calm. She's been binging her favorite show all morning, with Reese on FaceTime. Leo, also seems calmer than me.. but, a little more jittery than Q and Reese. I suppose everyone handles excitement in their own ways.. perhaps I wouldn't be so jumpy if police protocol wasn't involved.

I just got out of a meeting with Dianne, she had to go over prom protocol with me. The "in case"'s, the "in the event of"'s, and the "legally"'s. She tried not to make me nervous, but, it's never an easy thing to talk about; however, before our meeting ended, she told me not to worry and to have a good time.

What else? Well, graduation is coming quickly, and I still have some inward questions about valedictorian, like, if I'm not it.. and Quinn does decide to reject it, then, who does it go to? Valedictorian would've looked impeccable on a college application, but, maybe that doesn't matter. I've put college on the shelf for now, with the mini tour and all.. and, as long as my parents okay it, my plan will stay that way.

Speaking of plans, the hearing is the Monday before graduation.. so.. hopefully that's not gonna be too awkward; we should all be able to be adult about this. Dianne promised me that Mrs. Shay couldn't hold back my graduation because of this, so, there really shouldn't be a problem.

On a lighter note, we're gonna start getting ready in an hour, prom is from 8-11, we're gonna go to dinner at 6, so, 5 seems like a reasonable time to start hair and makeup. I'm so excited!

"Q!", *Brylee, somewhat calmly, exclaimed.*

"B!", *she replied in the same tone, never taking her eyes off the tv screen.*

"Do you think if we start getting ready at 5, we'll have enough time?".

"Yes.".

"Are you sure?".

"Yes.".

"Really sure?".

"Bry.", *Quinn paused her show, told Reese she'd call him back, and turned toward Brylee,* "How long does it usually take you to do your makeup?".

"I don't know, like, 10/15 minutes, maybe.", *she replied in deep thought.*

"Okay, How long does it take you to do you hair when we're going out somewhere?".

"Like, 25/30 minutes, or less, I think.", *she nodded as she spoke.*

"Good. Now, how long does it take you to put on a dress and slip into heels?".

"Definitely 7 minutes or less.", *Brylee chuckled.*

"Exactly.", *Quinn chuckled with slightly widened eyes, and a forced smirk,* "So, let's add. 15+30+7 equals?".

"It's 52 minutes, right?".

"Right. So, you could potentially be done getting ready at 5:52… is that cutting it too close for you?", *Quinn asked.*

"Yes.", *Bry decisively responded.*

"So.. what would be a better start time?", *Q tried pushing her brain to generate an answer.*

"Probably 4:45ish.", *B decided.*

"Good. So..", *Quinn shifted her gaze back to the tv and grabbed the remote,* "In one episode of "Vacation Mysteries", we'll get ready. Deal?".

"Deal.", *Bry smiled and sat next to Quinn on the bed.*

"Are you gonna call Reese back?", *Brylee asked.*

"Nah, I texted him and let him know that we're starting prom pregame, this is part of it.", *she pressed play and pulled her blanket over her.*

As the girls were "pregaming", their parents were having a meeting in the other room. Quinn's parents want to fly out to surprise her for graduation, so, Bryan and KaraLee figured they'd better catch them up on their daughter's life before they were sent into shock.

"Daniel! Kim! It's so nice to see your faces again, what's it been? A year?", *Bryan greeted them enthusiastically, over video chat.*

"Yes, well, you know we're very busy. The medical field never rests.", *Daniel dryly responded,* "In fact, it won't be resting during graduation either, but, Kim, the soft-heart that she is, insisted we fly out.".

Prom, and Maybe More

"Well, I have to agree with Kim, Quinn's graduation is a once in a lifetime experience.. you wouldn't want to miss it.", *KaraLee cut in.*

"Eh. Call me when she graduates college with a PhD.", *just then, Daniel's phone began to ring,* "Work, if you'll excuse me. Someone's life may depend on this very call.", *he got up and walked into the other room.*

"So, Kim! You're excited, right?", *KaraLee asked.*

"So-so.", *Kim replied, almost as dryly as her husband, however, she wouldn't look up from texting.*

"I have some new things to share with you about Quinn.. some things we should discuss, a few things we actually need your permission for.", *Bryan started,* "So—

"Oh!", *Kim exclaimed, cutting him off,* "Speaking of permission, I overnighted you some documents. You guys see Quinn more than we do, know her better than we do.. you basically have raised her as we've worked in the field —

"What are you getting at? What documents?", *KaraLee interrupted.*

Suddenly, Daniel appeared in front of the camera once again and took a seat.

"Guardianship papers.", *Daniel blurted as if it was obvious and no big deal.*

"Guardianship papers?!", *Kara exclaimed while letting out a small chuckle,* "She's almost 18, Dan.".

"Please, it's Daniel.".

"Sorry. Daniel, she's almost eighteen.", *KaraLee corrected herself in a slightly dimmed tone.*

"Right, so it seems, unnecessary, we understand.", *Kim took over the conversation once again,* "But, she will need certain permissions until then. We rarely talk to her! So, we feel that the permissions shouldn't be ran by us; these things should be decided by the people who truly know her.".

Bryan leaned over and began whispering to his wife.

"Kara, don't fight it. This is best, so let's agree before they change their minds.", *Bryan lingered for a moment, looking into her eyes, waiting for the information to sink in.*

"Okay.", *KaraLee said to Quinn's parents,* "You're right, and we're more than happy to take full responsibility for her.".

"Good. I knew you'd agree.", *Kim smiled from her eyes,* "Now, we have to go. We love you guys, always, for taking care of our daughter, the papers should be there sometime tonight according to the tracking. All you have to do is sign, then we'll finalize it while we're in town.".

"Wait. Is that the real reason you're coming to town? To finalize these papers?", *Kara asked with slight attitude in her tone.*

"Yes.", *Daniel replied as he took another call.*

"Wow.", *Bryan muttered under his breath.*

"You guys have to understand, as a doctor—

"You don't have the time to love the children that you bring into the world?", *KaraLee replied, getting emotional as Bryan rubbed her back, trying to momentarily calm her down.*

"We have to look for 2 birds, 1 stone opportunities.", *Kim replied unfazed.*

Not even a second after her reply, her phone started ringing.

"Okay, I have to go. Thank you for your cooperation! Bye.", *she hung up their call.*

Kara just sat there, in shock, wondering how a parent could do that to their child. Bryan began to speak, comforting her, as if he could read her every thought.

"Baby, I know that was hard to hear.. but, why was is so hard to hear?", *he asked as she looked up at him*, "Because, we consider her our own, and we have for a long time, Kay.".

"You're right.", *she sighed*, "At least now we don't have to worry about convincing them about anything, we can just make our own decisions, and that's that.".

"Exactly.", *Bryan smiled*, "We should actually be celebrating!".

"We should?", *she giggled.*

"Oh yeah, big time!", *Bryan began cheering her up*, "I see cake, champagne, dinner, a suit and tie.. oh, and what's that? This just in, you in your old prom dress.", *he smirked, wondering if he was about to get away with that.*

"We'll see.", *she rolled her eyes as she smiled and blushed.*

"I love you KaraLee Brown.", *Bryan kissed her nose.*

"I love you too, Mr. Bryan Brown.", *she closed her eyes and smiled.*

As they began walking out of their bedroom, KaraLee quickly turned and placed her hand on Bryan's chest, to stop him from walking any further.

"Quinn is not to know about any of this.", *her tone was serious, almost threatening, and her eyebrow was raised.*

"Agreed, Mama Bear.", *Bryan smiled with his eyebrows lifted.*

"We have to intercept that package before Quinn sees it, otherwise, she's gonna start asking about it.", *she warned.*

"That won't be a problem, you have to sign for things like that, they'll need us at the door.", *Bryan assured her.*

"Okay, good.", *she took a breath of relief and walked through the door.*

Meanwhile, it's 4:50 and the girls are finally getting ready, the first thing Bryan and KaraLee heard when they left their room was the girl's music blasting.

"My. Ears.", *Bryan teased, in a monotone voice.*

"It's prom night! Don't be an old man!", *his wife smiled as her mind reminisced.*

Time finally began to fly while the girls worked on their glamour. Their hair was in curlers as they did their makeup, and their curls were taking time to relax as they steamed their dresses. It's a good thing they started before 5, cuz their pregame, of course, involved dancing around the room and singing into their makeup brushes. As the clock ticked closer to 6, their hearts started pounding, and they couldn't keep random parts of their body from shaking. It was all becoming so real.

At 5:45, Bryan heard a knock at the door; he opened it to find Leo and Reese standing there, dazzling. He welcomed them in and KaraLee began taking endless pictures.

"Boysssss! You look so handsome!!", *she exclaimed as she continued the photoshoot.*

"Thank you, Mrs. Brown.", *they smiled and tried to hide their blushing.*

"Don't be weird, it's Bryan and KaraLee.", *Bryan said as he put his arms around the boys, getting in the next picture.*

As they were discussing the rules for the night, the girl's music suddenly shut off.

"Sounds like pregame is over.", *Reese chuckled, looking over at Leo.*

"You guys ready to catch a preview of your future brides?", *Bryan teased, only, he truly meant it.*

"Absolutely.", *Leo replied confidently, while keeping his eyes glued to the hallway they were about to emerge from.*

Everyone's attention shifted to the beauties entering the room. The sound of sharp stilettos tapping the tile announced their entrance. As they came was *into view, everyone was speechless, stunned, starstruck. The boy's eyes widened and sparkled as they caught their love's attention. The girls glimmered and shined from head to toe, their intense beauty flooded the atmosphere, becoming the only thing they could breathe in, in that moment. The silence was broken by Quinn, of course.*

"So, we look good, right?", *Quinn poked.*

"Very.", *Reese smiled.*

They walked into the living room where everyone was, and met their dates; KaraLee was, of course, taking more pictures. The boys spent a little more time staring at their ladies, taking it all in, as they put their corsages on them, and as the girls placed their boutonnières perfectly.

"Wow, you put that on like a professional.", *Leo commented, slightly surprised, considering the florist told him that he might get stabbed a few times.*

"Well, I've been practicing since I was little.", *Bry looked into his eyes and let out a soft giggle,* "On teddy bears, obviously.", *she patted his chest, signaling that he was good to go.*

"Obviously.", *he teased, as he smiled at her.*

"Girls! Get next to your dates! I want some pictures.", *Kara exclaimed, while motioning them to move in closer.*

They crowded in and smiled for the camera; the photoshoot dragged on until Bryan stepped in.

"Okay, I think you've got enough to last a lifetime.", *he chuckled as he slowly lowered his wife's phone.*

"Fine. I suppose you're right.", *she playfully squinted at him.*

"We better get going, guys.", *Reese announced to the group,* "Reservation is for 6:15.".

"Okay! Just one more picture, one more!", *Kara lifted her phone once more.*

"Okay, guys, you better get out of here. Go, before you spend prom night in your mother's photoshoot.", *he practically pushed the kids out the door.*

"Okay! Have fun, y'all!", *KaraLee shouted as they walked out the door.*

Bryan shut the door, and looked at his wife.

"What?", *she asked.*

"Think you have enough pictures?", *he teased.*

"No.".

Bryan shook his head and smiled.

"Should we start the celebration?", *he asked.*

"We should.", *she replied with an excited smile.*

While they were beginning their night, the kids were beginning theirs. As they were making their way to their car, they were stopped by a man.

"Excuse me!", *he shouted.*

Everyone stopped where they were and turned around.

"Any of you by chance a member of the brown residence?".

"Who's asking?", *Reese protectively quizzed.*

"USPS.".

"Oh! Yes, I'm a resident.", *Brylee replied.*

Prom, and Maybe More

"Do you happen to have I.D. on you?".

Brylee pulled her license from her clutch, and offered it to the man.

"Perfect, Sign here, please.".

He handed her a pen and a clipboard, and she signed.

"Here you go.".

He handed her a package, then left. Everyone got in the car, once they were settled, she read the package.

"Quinn, it's from your parents, here.".

She handed the envelope over.

Chapter 22

PARTIES, PACKAGES, AND POLICE

A short drive later, they made it to the venue. It was completely different from Brylee's designs, how Jenny made so many changes in so little time, she'll never know, but, rather than wallowing, she decided to find the beauty in it. There were lights everywhere, she actually did a really good job, it was like a little slice of Italy hidden in Friday Harbor. There were fountains, cobblestone streets, and a beautiful bridge, toward the back, overlooking the city. It was absolutely mesmerizing, the perfect location.

The theme, of course, was "Little Italy", the ballroom was a corner of Europe, and all the foods were decadent; the music was classic; it was like a 3 hour tour of the sights. There were intricate paintings on the walls, gold infused pillars, and marble vases filled with white flowers dusted in silver. It wasn't what I planned, but, somehow, it was better.

I couldn't wait to rush inside, I pulled Leo along with me to start exploring; however, Quinn stayed in the car to open the package.

"You sure you don't want me to wait for you?", *Reese asked.*

"I'm sure.", *Quinn assured him,* "It's not often that my parents send packages, it's probably for graduation, I want to open it in private.".

"Okay, I understand. Remember, if you need me, I'm here. I'll be watching the door, so I can come get you when you get inside.. okay?".

"Okay, thanks Newb.", *Q gave him a soft smile.*

"Of course, Q-Tip, I love you.", *he replied with a smirk.*

"I love you too.", *her eyes sparkled in the moonlight as Reese shut the car door and headed inside the building.*

When she was sure that she was alone, she opened up the padded envelope; as she carefully tore into it, a million thoughts raced through her head: "Is it money?", "Is it keys to my own car?", "Is it my personal documents? I'm almost 18, I do need those.", "Is it a letter?". *She pulled the contents out and looked at them slightly perplexed.*

"Definitely documents...", *she whispered to herself while examining them.*

She flipped through the packet seeing x's and yellow and pink highlighter in peculiar places, as she neared the end of the documents, a letter fell into her lap. She picked it up and found that it was actually addressed to Brylee's parents. She quickly grabbed the envelope and saw that it too was addressed to them.

"Ugh. Leave it to Brylee to accidentally assist in a federal offense.", *Quinn sighed.*

She closed the packet and began carefully placing the papers back inside their packaging; however, she grew too curious to simply put the letter back, so, she took it upon herself to read it. While she was skimming the note, Reese, Leo, and Brylee were inside stuffing their faces.

"Quinns been out there a while, why don't you go get her?", *Bry spoke to Reese with a mouth full of pastry.*

"She wanted to be alone, I want to respect that. I'll give it 15 more minutes, if she still hasn't come inside, I'll go check on her.", *he replied.*

"Fair enough. You're a good guy, I'm glad she's with you.", *she nodded at him in approval,* "And you!", *she turned to Leo,* "You're a good guy too, and I'm glad I'm with you.", *she smirked.*

"Truly, the pleasure is all mine, M'ilady.", *Leo lifted her hand and kissed it, making her blush,* "Would you care for a dance?".

"I would love to dance with you, sir.", *she giggled and took his hand.*

As they walked toward the dance floor, Leo looked back at Reese.

"You gonna be okay over there alone, Bruv?".

"Yeah.", *Reese chuckled,* "Don't worry, my dance card is full.".

Bry and Leo began their dance, and Reese started on his 4th piece of pizza; as he bit in, Quinn caught his eye. She walked through the door, but, this time, the only thing glimmering was her dress in the dancing lights. Her face was dim, and her eyes cried out in distress. Immediately, Reese threw his pizza down and rushed over to her, cleaning his hands on the way. She saw him coming closer, and felt a certain weight lift off her shoulders, however, instead of walking forward to meet him, she stayed planted where she was, waiting for him to reach her.

"Hey, what's the matter?", *Reese asked, notably concerned.*

"The package wasn't meant for me.", *she somberly replied.*

"But, Bry said it was from your parents.".

"Yeah, and it was, but, it was addressed to her parents.".

"Are you sad that it wasn't for you?", *he tried to understand why she was so upset.*

"No. That doesn't phase me anymore.", *she admitted.*

As they continued their conversation, Brylee happened to see Quinn from over Leo's shoulder, mid dance. There she was, twirling, floating on cloud 9, having the time of her life, and, there was her best friend, looking like she had just received the most horrid news of her life.

"Leo.", *Brylee whispered, still looking over his shoulder at every turn.*

"Love.", *he replied, matching her tone.*

He dipped her, smiling into her eyes before bringing her back to earth. As he brought her back up, he noticed the look on her face.

"What's the matter? Is it my dancing?", *he poked, trying to lighten the mood.*

"Look.", *she stopped dancing and nodded in Quinn's direction,* "She looks like she's gonna cry.".

"Do you want to go see what the matter is?", *he kindly asked.*

"Honestly, yes. I'm sorry to disrupt the night, but I want to be able to have fun, and—

Leo cut her frantic explanation short, by gently tilting her chin up so he could make eye contact with his very distracted date.

"Darling, I understand. There's plenty of time still to dance, let's go make sure your best friend is okay first.".

He took her hand and led her through the dancing crowd to the front doors that Quinn and Reese were beginning to walk out of. On their way out, Bry squeezed Leo's hand as to say, "Thank you.", he turned and smiled at her as he held the door open for her; when they got outside, they saw Q and Reese leaned up against the bridge talking. Bry immediately ran over.

"Quinn! What's wrong?!", *she exclaimed in concern.*

"Nothing, really, I'm okay. Don't pause prom on my account! Go! We'll be in in a sec.", *she replied, trying to convince her friend that nothing traumatic happened.*

"I'm not buyin' it. Number 1, I know you. Number 2, you were as excited as I was about this then you— you stayed behind to open the package! That's what's wrong, isn't it?! What was in it???", *Bry started calm, but began shouting as she put together the puzzle like Sherlock Holmes.*

"The package wasn't actually for me, B.".

"What do you mean? Who else would your parents send a package to a week before graduation?", *Brylee retorted, puzzled.*

"Your parents.".

"My parents? Why? OH NO! I didn't ruin some sort of surprise, did I?!".

"Wellll, I mean, to a certain extent.", *Reese mumbled in a pitchy tone.*

Brylee looked at Reese with her eyebrows tilted in concern, then quickly looked back at Quinn, as if she was asking, "Is that true?!".

"No. You didn't ruin a surprise.", *Quinn reclaimed Bry's attention.*

"So, then, why are you so upset? Don't worry, my parents won't report you for opening their mail—well, maybe they'll tell Mrs. D.", *she teased.*

Quinn forced a small laugh.

"Are you gonna tell her, or should I?", *Reese looked at Q,* "This has to be talked about.".

"What?! Quinn! You already know you can tell me anything!!!", *B exclaimed in frustration.*

"I know.".

"Then, why aren't you telling me?".

"MY PARENTS ARE SIGNING THEIR RIGHTS TO ME OVER TO YOUR PARENTS, basically! Cuz apparently it's too hard for them to be doctors and a parent at the same time.".

Quinn pulled the crumpled note from her pocket and handed it to Brylee; she quickly skimmed it, and so did Leo from over her shoulder.

"I'm sorry for raising my voice.", *Q apologized,* "It's just... kinda wack. Like, lowkey, I'm wondering if anyone would've told me, or if they were just gonna keep it from me.".

"I imagine that my parents at least would've told you.. or, maybe not, they probably didn't want to upset you, especially tonight.", *Bry continued,* "I don't know if you're ready for the bright side, but, there is one, and I want to show you.".

"I'm listening.", *Quinn quipped.*

"Okay, so, as harsh as this probably sounds, your parents may not have the time to be parents, which, shouldn't come as a shock, they've never had time.. that's why you've basically always lived with me, and my parents ARE your parents; BUT, nonetheless, yours still love you. Are they more of, like, your donors? Yes! And even though it might kinda hurt that they're making it 'official' as if they didn't already all those years ago, pretty much, your life stays they same, EXCEPT, they don't get to make any of your decisions, WHICH MEANS, you have a better chance at going on tour, AND, getting married to Reese whenever you want. What they're signing over is their right to judge you, and parent you; they aren't signing away their right to love you.", *Brylee explained.*

Q was crying at this point, Reese was comforting her, and Leo had a single hand on her shoulder as a sign of support. She began shaking her head and smiling, which, for a minute, confused them all.

"What would I do without you?", *Quinn exhaled.*

She launched at Brylee, nearly knocking her to the ground, and wrapped her arms tightly around her.

"You're right, every word of it, facts. Thank you. It's true what they say, who you surround yourself with matters.", *Q momentarily pulled away so she could look at her best friend,* "You help me to not slip into that old, bitter Quinn that doesn't know how to love. You help me to be a better me, always, and I can't thank you enough.", *she latched onto her once more,* "You, and your parents are my chosen family, Bry.".

"You're my chosen family too, Quinn. We all love you, so much.", *Brylee looked at the boys and motioned them to join.*

"Hey, don't forget about us!", *Leo once again began lightening up the mood, as he hugged them both.*

"Yeah, I love you, baby.. you're my chosen family too.", *Reese assured her as he joined the hug.*

Quinn began to laugh, and wipe her tears as she broke out of the group hug.

"Thank you, guys. I love you all.. this little group IS a chosen family.", *she endearingly announced.*

"Forever.", *Leo agreed.*

"And eternity.", *Reese added in a cheesy tone.*

"Don't worry, we won't sign over our rights to you.", *Bry teased.*

Quinn laughed and rolled her eyes.

"Thanks! I appreciate that!", *she laughed as Reese put his suit jacket around her shoulders.*

"Leo, what? You're not gonna offer her your jacket? I'm always calling you 'the perfect gentleman'.", *Q quipped.*

"In fact, I was going to, but, she's hot to the touch.", *he replied, with slight surprise in his tone.*

Quinn looked at her friend, surprised, considering she's always cold.

"Adrenaline.", *she chuckled as she shrugged,* "Believe me, I'll need his jacket as soon as my fight or flight balances out.".

They all started laughing.

"So, should we head back inside?", *Leo asked.*

"Yes! Let's go!", *Quinn exclaimed, excited once again.*

They began walking back into the party, but were abruptly stopped by a psychopathic shout. They all whipped around to see what all the fuss was about, and, of course, the fuss was Jason. He was obviously drunk, stumbling more than he was actually walking, and aggressively shouting slurs of words, that seemed to make no sense at all.

His hair was a mess, his face looked greasy, his suit was sloppy, all signs of sobriety left him. Don't even ask where he got the alcohol, if you've watched any teen "coming of age" movie, you know that it's not that hard to sneak it in. His senses were dulled, there was no way he knew what he was doing; or, maybe he did.

"BrYlEe!", *her name fell like slime out of his babbling mouth.*

"Come on, Love, let's just go back into the party, the cops will deal with him.", *Leo softly commanded, as he placed his hand on her back and led her forward.*

She walked forward, following his lead, but couldn't help looking back to see what was happening behind her. As she watched him ramble on, she saw something that stopped her in her tracks and shook her to her very core.

"Leo, stop. Leo, Stop! Look!", *she frantically demanded as she shook her date's arm.*

Leo, along with Quinn and Reese, turned around to see that Jason climbed onto the ledge of the bridge, and was walking it like a tightrope, with his arms out for balance.

"What. Is. He. Doing?", *Leo sighed.*

"WHERE ARE THE COPS?", *Quinn raised her voice in desperate concern.*

"Leo, bro, do we do something?", *Reese asked, unsure of the protocol in a situation like this.*

He didn't answer them, he just kept his eyes locked on the target, studying him, to see what game he was playing.

"Leo, say something, please.", *Brylee asked with doe eyes.*

"He's seeking attention.", *he replied,* "Let's see what happens when he doesn't get any. Brylee.", *he turned and looked at her,* "He's looking to get a rise out of you.. don't give him the satisfaction.".

Bry nodded in agreement, composed herself, and put on a serious—slightly disinterested—face.

"Good.", *Leo stated,* "Reese, come with me, we need to get closer, just in case this thing takes a turn. Quinn, will you please stay here with Brylee?".

"Of course.", *Q nodded as she grabbed Bry's hand.*

Leo nodded in relief, and Reese kissed Quinn on the cheek before he walked away; as the boys got closer to the bridge, Jason got louder, attracting a small crowd.

"Oh, look who it is!", *Jason maniacally laughed,* "Well, if it isn't prince charmin', and his little skate-a boy!", *he mocked in a bad British accent as he continued to walk the ledge.*

Leo ignored him, hoping that he would get bored and come down.

"What's that? Can't hear me?", *he continued in his fake British,* "Perhaps your ears are filled with too much of that horrible singing; I mean, that was almost a deal breaker.".

Leo took a deep breath and chuckled like, "You have no idea what you're talking about.".

"She doesn't sing.", *Leo retorted.*

"No, I know, but that friend of hers does.", *he broke his fake accent and assumed his regular, drunken one.*

He side eyed Reese as he made that comment, trying to gauge a reaction, but, he got nothing.

"You know, Leo.. you're a reallyyy lucky guy.", *Jason momentarily stopped his tightrope walk so he could make eye contact with the man he couldn't stand,* "And, you're a reallyy good writer too. Too bad your girlfriend is such a smarty pants.. if she wasn't, she'd be with me right now.".

As he pivoted his foot to start walking again, he started to slip, but caught himself before he fell; while he was slipping, Brylee let out a yelp, and covered her mouth in horror. Leo sharply sighed, both at the close call, and the thought of his soon to come comments about Brylee.

"Did you hear that little yelp, Leo?", *he teased with disgust on his face,* "Sounds like your little lady DOES care what happens to me.", *his laughter picked up once again,* "I knew it.".

As his walk looped back around, it began to rain.

Parties, Packages, and Police

"How romantic!", *Jason exclaimed in a mocking tone,* "She always was a sucker for romance.", *he rolled his eyes, then squeezed them shut in pain, and shook his head.*

"Jason, get down from there, now.", *Leo demanded in a firm tone.*

As he began talking him down, Reese texted Dianne and their personal details to alert them.

"Why? What? Are ya worried?', *he mocked and picked up pace.*

"Jason, get down, now. It's raining, you're drunk.. don't do something that you'll regret—

"OH, BUT THAT'S JUST THE THING, PRINCE CHARMING!", *he cut Leo off with a rage filled scream,* "I ALREADY HAVE.".

The rain beat down harder and harder, moving Jason's hair in front of his eyes, and making the stone more slippery. The more he yelled, the more people he drew, which resulted in more police calls.

"JASON! Get. Down. Now.".

A familiar voice pushed through the crowd.

"Oh, I don't even wanna hear one single word out of you.", *he chuckled in resentment as he responded to Shay's voice,* "Some aunt you are.".

"Jason!", *she shouted.*

"SHUT UP!", *he crazily laughed,* "Just, shut up.", *he sighed.*

"Jason, it's my job to—

"WHAT?! What Shay? Your job to, what, protect me?", *he whipped around so he could see her as he was walking,* "This is all YOUR fault, YOUR idea! Remember?".

Mrs. Shay started to disappear into the crowd, which only riled Jason up.

"Oh, how heroic! You know, you talk all about protecting your students like baby birds, but what about your nephew?! Or, you wanna talk students? What about Brylee?!", *Jason shouted, stopping Shay in her tracks.*

At this point, the police were peppered into and around the crowd.

"Yeah, let's talk about 'The World's Best Principal'!", *he laughed*, "Let's talk about how you've had this planned since my 'episode' in front of the recruiter. Let's talk about how you HATE working with kids, so you wanted a big time athlete nephew, so you could retire early and chip away at my millions from the Maldives! Let's talk about how 'star student' was code, so I knew which student you were setting me up with. Let's talk about how you saw Leo leave that letter, so you erased his name and put mine instead. Let's talk about how you stalked Brylee and Quinn while they were shopping, and bought the perfect corsage to keep in your back pocket, for blackmail. Let's talk about how you signed into my Apple I.D. and how YOU were the one pressuring her to go to prom with me, and how you gaslit and scared her until she went to the cops. LET'S TALK ABOUT, how you took her address from school records, and forced me to go threaten her for you, of course, not without rehearsing your script first! Let's talk about how you made me bump into her in the hall at school, or, how you drove me to that baseball field just to scare her off. ANY OF THIS RING A BELL?!", *he shouted as he walked faster*, "Or, how about my personal favorite? "Jason, if you don't do this for me, I'll make sure you NEVER graduate or play another sport in your entire life.", well, you know what? I don't care about sports anymore.. not after seeing what they can push someone to do. Actually, it was greed.. greed and bitterness.".

Mrs. D had Shay handcuffed and ready to go, but, she forced her to stay and hear the speech.

"And why did she do it, ladies and gentlemen?", *Jason looked out at the crowd*, "'Because recruiters pick the boys who are promising. What boy is more promising than one who has a good, grounded girl?'", *he made eye contact with Shay, then looked in Brylee's direction*, "I'm sorry.", *he shouted*, "For everything, Brylee.".

Brylee and Quinn walked over to Leo and Reese once it seemed safe enough, they put their arms around their date's shoulders; Leo put his jacket around Brylee.

"Can you prove it?", *Mrs. D asked Jason.*

"I'll turn over my phone as evidence, the conversations are all there.", *he replied.*

"Oh, I'm sure gonna enjoy this.", *Dianne smirked and handed Shay off to another cop,* "Read her her rights and put her in a car.", *she demanded,* "Ima make sure you neva hurt anotha child again.. EVA.", *she promised.*

While everyone was distracted with the arrest, crowd control, and the party, Jason got in jumping position; as he dangled a foot over the edge, Brylee caught a glimpse and shrieked again, drawing everyone's attention back to him.

"JASON?! What are you doing?!", *Brylee screamed.*

"Well, to be honest, I don't really feel like dancing.", *he quipped, slightly more sober than earlier, but, still drunk.*

He alluded to jumping again, he was prepared to take a fall he would not come back from. The policemen that are experienced in talking people down tried to get close to him, but, it only provoked him and encouraged him to jump. Reese took control, and made the cops back up, earning Jason's trust. He began talking him down, and once he was distracted enough, Leo launched, and tackled him strategically off the bridge, and landed him on the cobblestone sidewalk. Jason started shaking and crying, every ounce of alcohol was knocked out of his system. Reese helped him and Leo up, and Quinn and Brylee came a bit closer.

"Why did, you, out of all people help me?", *Jason wept,* "I stole your note, threatened your girl.. why wouldn't you let me jump?".

"A note isn't worth your life. I don't care what you've done to me, I'm not gonna stand by and watch you end it all. Besides, there was, evidently, more to the story.", *Leo continued,* "I forgive you, even for what you did to Brylee; but I want you to stay away from her. You need to sober up, man, and you need some help.".

Hearing that, made Brylee decide to also forgive him, she decided to let go of her bitterness and disgust, and riskily, walked over and gave Jason a genuine hug; which made him cry even harder.

"Why did you do that?", *Jason asked her.*

"Because, I forgive you.", *she replied.*

She walked away as the police took Jason into custody, and met up with Quinn.

"Hey.. I'm sorry for how I've been acting about the valedictorian thing.", *Bry apologized once more.*

"Of course, I forgive you, we already handled that!", *Q grabbed her hand,* "That was real brave what you did—forgiving Jason like that.".

"It's what was right.", *Brylee admitted,* "I did it for me, un-forgiveness would've just hurt me in the end.".

"Looks like Leo is a good influence on you.", *Quinn chuckled.*

Leo and Reese came over to the girls and gave them all the information they collected. Apparently, Jason was being admitted into the psych ward which automatically puts the restraining order into motion, without a court date. That meant, they only needed their secret service for one more night, and Bry didn't have to worry about appearing in court. She felt a weight lift of he shoulders, and she started dancing.

"What are you doing?", *Leo laughed.*

Quinn looked at him with a funny face, turned on her and Bry's favorite song, then joined in. Not even a second later, the boys joined in and they all danced there on the sidewalk, in the pouring rain, until every person and vehicle cleared out, but them. Once it was empty, they decided they'd better get going too.

"Anyone else hungry?", *Reese asked as they were walking to the car.*

"Yes!", *Leo agreed.*

"My favorite part of prom was the pizza.", *Reese poked.*

"What was your favorite part, B?", *Quinn asked.*

"Dancing with you in the rain.", *she replied with a smile.*

Prom in the Rain

Chapter 23

RECOVERY

Fast forward to the night before graduation; so much has happened in the last few days. There's been a lawsuit filed against Mrs. Shay, after a little more digging, Dianne found that she's done shady things at 3 other schools, and the parents, students, and staff are willing to come forward and testify against her. Jason has a lessened sentence, 2 months in psychiatric care, 2 months in jail on watch—for his part in the scheme— then 3 months free, on probation, with therapy.

Quinn's parents are here, and they've been here for 2 days already.. it was a rocky start, but, I'd say the atmosphere has improved. My parents were SHOOK when Q handed them the already opened envelope, filled with official documents—speechless, really— but, Quinn quickly assured them that she understood; in fact, we had a little celebration, with the guys, and her favorite desserts, all things Quinn. Then came her parents, I thought it was really gonna stir something up in her, but, amazingly enough, her parents were the only ones stirring something up.

She patiently listened to their manipulative explanations, nodded along, assured them she wasn't mad; then, when they still wouldn't let it go, she looked them in the eyes and said, "I forgive you, both of you.". They had no idea what to say, that amount of love just put a cork in their mouths; but Q didn't leave it at that, she shocked them even more with a hug, then she walked away. I was so proud; she said that with all the forgiveness going around, it just felt right.

Our parents got the papers signed, filed, and finalized—it's official! Quinn belongs to us! Oh, sorry, sorry, I forgot, she wants me to stop saying that—it makes her feel like a stray dog— it doesn't help that once it was all finalized I shouted, "SO WE GET TO KEEP HER?!". I thought it was funny.. so did Reese, and my dad, to be honest, BUT,

I promised I'd stop saying it. It's my adoption gift to her—oh— she wants me to stop saying that too. ANYWAYS... it all worked out great!

We are BEYOND excited, tomorrow, not only do we graduate, BUT, we get an answer about the tour. I'm hoping that all these forgiveness testimonies prove maturity and responsibility. I don't know how we're gonna sleep tonight.. we actually might not sleep at all—no, no— never-mind, we have to sleep. However, we probably won't go to bed till late; our parents are letting the boys sleep over, I feel like they're trying to see what we'd do on the tour bus. Anyways, we're binging movies, and snacking, a lot; but, come bedtime, it's me and Q in our room, and the boys in the living room, so, not to worry.

Also, our parents, and I mean, all 4, have been out "shopping", morning to night, every day since Dan and Kim have arrived, yet, they never come home with anything. I say it's sus, Quinn seems to think they're actually planning a grad party; of course, the adults deny that it's sus, and that it's a party; in fact, my dad denied that it was a "sus party", so, it's probably a sus party.

Our secret service fell off the morning after the prom incident, but, Mrs. D still checks in on all of us; she's actually coming to graduation! I'm pretty excited about that, she feels like an auntie at this point.. she literally told us to start calling her Auntie D, she definitely makes up for the broken relationship with Shay. I asked her not to come in uniform, but, I have a feeling, at the very least, her badge, gun, and taser will be under her dress; which is fine, I mean, according to Quinn, "It pays to know cops.", whatever that means.

So, through all this, I've learned about true forgiveness, love, and self control. I've seen the effects of bitterness, and decided that I never want to let that take root. I've gained 3 new family members, Leo, Reese, and Auntie D; and it's always cool to have more people to love you. I learned that it's okay if something isn't in my control, and when you let go, things turn out better than you can imagine. I learned that titles aren't everything, and that it doesn't matter what others think of you; and I think Quinn would agree.

If I had the choice to do this all again, I wouldn't change the journey that lead me to wholeness.

"It's been a wild end of the year, hasn't it?", *Quinn commented as she put popcorn in the microwave.*

"Indeed, it has.", *Leo agreed.*

"Yeah, but, I'm glad it happened; no offense, Bry.", *Reese said as he chewed on a twizzler.*

"None taken.", *Brylee chuckled.*

"It's just that, look how we were all brought together.. it's pretty cool.", Reese looked around at everyone, "I mean, I don't know about you, but, I didn't have many—

"Any!", *Quinn fake coughed.*

"Any.", *Reese jokingly side eyed her*, "Friends—no friends. I was praying for you guys, and I didn't even know it. Now I have, 2 friends, a second family, and a much more than friend.", *he teased Quinn at the end.*

"I totally agree.", *Brylee chimed in as she plopped down on the couch*, "Jesus totally presented me with so many opportunities, and taught me so many things. Like, I could've been so scared of men after Jason, but, I believe He sent Leo into my pathway directly after so fear didn't have time to set in. He's even used Leo to draw me closer to Him in certain ways.".

"Yeah, I experienced that too. Leo is the one who first told me about Jesus; it was during all the stuff happening with my parents last year, and little did I know, he introduced me to my True Love; Who I believe introduced me to my earth love.", *Quinn admitted.*

"Earth love?", *Reese chuckled.*

"You like it.", *Quinn teased.*

"That I do.".

"Maybe we should try telling Jason about Him. I mean, we have testimonies for a reason, right?", *Leo suggested.*

"We should definitely pray about it, cuz one things for sure, Jason needs Jesus.", *Quinn replied.*

"Quinn!", *Bry exclaimed.*

"What?! It's true!", *she giggled.*

"Okay, okay—SO— what are we gonna watch??", *Reese asked as he grabbed the remote.*

"Rom-com?", *Bry suggested.*

"Action!", *Q blurted.*

"Suspense.", *Reese shook his head.*

"Comedy—obviously— I mean, who doesn't want to laugh?", *Leo settled the matter.*

"True.", *Reese responded.*

"Alright, how about, we watch 1 movie from all 4 genres.", *Brylee suggested, satisfied with her solution.*

"Okay, fair.", *Quinn agreed.*

As soon as the first movie began, all the parents came out to say goodnight.

"Make sure you guys get some sleep!", *Kim exclaimed.*

"We will ma-ma.", *Q replied.*

"Don't go to bed too late.", *Bryan gently commanded as he kissed the girl's heads.*

"And remember, separate rooms!", *KaraLee shouted the reminder as she rounded the corner toward her bedroom.*

"Yes, ma'am!", *the boys shouted in agreement.*

"Girls.", *They heard Bryan from down the hall, demanding that they also agree.*

"We understand!", *the girls shouted.*

Once silence returned, they resumed their movie, and continued their celebration.

Chapter 24

GRADUATION

Here it finally is! Graduation day!!! I don't know about the boys, but, we were aiming to sleep in; however, we were awaked by the mixed aromas of bacon, coffee, donuts, potatoes, eggs, syrup, whipped cream, toast—the works— by the time we stumbled out of our room, Leo and Reese were on their second plates.

"Come, come!", *Bryan welcomed the girls,* "There's plenty! We made all your favorites!!".

They took their usual seats at the counter, and started piling up their plates. Bry first went for the donuts, Quinn, of course, went for the bacon.

"Here's your usuals.", *KaraLee set their coffees down in front of them.*

"You know our usuals?", *Quinn asked as she sipped on her iced coffee.*

While Kara was gonna go with an endearing nod and smile, Bryan just couldn't help himself.

"It's hard to miss when y'all are dancing around the kitchen at 5 a.m. yelling your orders like baristas.", *he teased, as a dad would.*

"We don't dAnce around at 5 a.m.", *Bry replied, blushing, slightly embarrassed.*

"Yeah, it's more like 6:30.", *Quinn played along.*

"And, I don't yell— that early.", *Brylee attempted to save face.*

"You're right, actually, you don't— she doesn't, guys.", *he looked over at the boys,* "It's more like singing.".

He chuckled as he flipped an egg.

"That's pretty cute.", *Leo softly chuckled as he brought his coffee mug to his lips.*

"And here I was thinking Quinn was the only musical one in this house.", *Reese poked.*

"Okay, okay. Yes, I sing and dance in the mornings. The cat is out of the bag.", *she teased herself in embarrassment.*

"Don't be embarrassed, I sing in the shower.", *KaraLee joined in.*

"Oh, we know!", *Bryan, Quinn, and Brylee exclaimed all at once.*

Kara smiled and rolled her eyes as she set more donuts out.

"So, we have a surprise for you—all of you— and it's from all us parents, all 4 of us.", *Bryan said as he grabbed his coffee.*

"Is it, by chance, an answer?", *Quinn quipped.*

"Nice try, Quinny.", *Bryan smiled,* "It's better than just an answer.".

"So, when do we get to open it?", *Bry asked, excitedly.*

"It isn't wrapped.", *Kim spoke calmly as her and her husband took a seat at the counter.*

"Good morning mom, and dad.", *Q greeted them as her mom rubbed her back.*

"So, are we supposed to guess, or?", *Reese asked.*

"Yeah, you've given us clues, are we supposed to put it together like a puzzle?", *Leo inquired.*

"I guess we'll see.", *KaraLee mysteriously replied.*

"Nice one, mom.", *Brylee started,* "I hope I don't trip and fall on stage cuz I'm thinking about this.".

"I hope not either, honey.", *her mom replied, unfazed and fully aware that she was just trying to get an answer out of her.*

"Speaking of grad, I'm gonna go take a nap; we have to leave in a couple hours, and, I'm pretty tired from last night.", *Reese admitted.*

"Me too, honestly.", *Leo agreed.*

"We should probably rest too, Q.", *Bry looked at her friend who looked half asleep.*

"I blame the bacon.", *Quinn replied in a daze.*

"Ah, yes, the meat, not the 2 a.m. bedtime.", *Brylee teased.*

"Precisely.", *Quinn smiled really big, then walked off to their room without saying another word.*

"Yep, she's tired.", *Bry chuckled,* "See you all in a couple hours.".

The kids all went their separate ways, while the adults fellowshipped in the kitchen, reflecting on how quickly their babies grew up.

"Can you believe they're about to be graduated adults?", *Kara asked.*

"It's crazy.", *Kim replied,* "I still remember that day in second grade when they met; who knew that they'd still be going strong?".

"Who knew they'd eventually stop thinking that boys have coodies?", *Bryan pretended to tear up.*

"We all knew.", *KaraLee smiled and shook her head.*

"I'm with you, Bryan.", *Daniel lifted his coffee cup as to say,* "cheers".

"Dads.", *Kim shook her head at Kara and laughed.*

The hours seemed to fly by as everybody enjoyed life, and soon, it was time to get to the school. The kids were ready, all dressed up in their cap and gowns; and heading through the door. They felt like 4 ready adults, their parents felt like they were 4 second graders about to surf the waves of life; like any parent does on graduation day. They were all teary eyed as the kids smiled and laughed, but excited about this next phase. As they crowded into the car, Quinn spoke up.

"Wait!".

"What?!", *Kim frantically replied,* "Why are you shouting?!".

"You get used to it.", *Bryan assured her.*

"I forgot my guitar!!!", *Q exclaimed.*

"Why do you need your—

Before Daniel could get his question out, Quinn leapt from the car, ran into the house, grabbed her guitar, ran back, and threw it in the trunk.

"Electric?", *Reese asked as she settled back into her seat.*

"You know it.".

"Nice.", *he nodded in approval.*

"What do you have planned?", *Bry whispered.*

"You'll see.", *Q smirked in reply.*

Chapter 25

EVERYTHING ELSE

They arrived right on time for the opening speech given by the vice principal, found seats right next to each other, and readied their phones to record the special moment. The students weren't sitting in the same area as the parents, they were at the front, in a group, and the parents were in the back. As they sat, just waiting, Brylee grew nervous.

"Brylee, breathe, it's okay.", *Quinn reminded her.*

"I know, thank you, I'm not freaking out, don't worry.", *she assured her.*

"I know.", *Q smiled, alerting Leo, with her eyes, to keep tabs on Bry.*

Directly after the speech came an announcement, the group knew exactly what was coming next. It was time to announce this year's valedictorian. As the announcement was made, Brylee appeared to be unbothered, and quickly, a large smile overtook her face as Quinn was called to the stage. She got up, confidently, and headed over with her guitar.

"What's she doing with her guitar?", *Leo whispered.*

"We'll see.", *Reese smiled wide with his phone in the air, recording what he knew was about to be a wild moment.*

Quinn shook the vice principal's hand and allowed him to drape the valedictorian shawl over her shoulders, before taking the microphone. As she started talking, she began giggling at the shocked faces of her parents.

"I see many of you are surprised!", *she chuckled,* "No offense taken, I get it!", *she put her guitar strap over her shoulder and began to tune it,* "My speech isn't gonna be traditional, by the way, in case you couldn't tell. I have a long reveal, I've been working on it for a while, sometimes in class.".

Reese chuckled, remembering the day he got the courage to talk to her.

"So, here it goes.", *Quinn started playing,*

"Known you since grade 2,

Don't know what I would do without you;

Luckily, I don't have to,

Livin' everyday next to you.

You're right,

That thing you said last night,

I can see that twinkle in your eyes;

Just like I did when we were kids,

After we promised.

We'd never be apart,

Best friends to the end and at the start,

Forever a piece of my heart;

Adventures under the stars,

I'll bring my guitar.

I won't run away,

When times get hard,

I'd rather prom in the rain with you,

Than starin' out my window wonderin'

Where you are and if you're coming back soon;

So it's settled,

I've made my decision,

You'll always be a part of my vision.

Dancing in the wet grass,

Heels in our hands,

Underneath the stadium lights,

I'd rather prom in the rain with you,

Than a million perfect nights with a stranger.

Prom in the rain is just our flavor.

Tailor made,

Lemonade,

Ice cold breeze on a hot hot day,

Strawberries,

You and me,

Singing along to this melodyyyy.

Remember when we danced all night?

Muddy feet and shredded dresses,

Shuffled all our favorite albums,

While we were backlit by the moon;

We didn't have a curfew,

Nothing holding us back,

That's when I said,

That's when I said:

I won't run away,

When times get hard;

I'd rather prom in the rain with you,

Than starin' out my window wonderin'

Where you are and if you're coming back soon;

So it's settled,

I've made my decision,

You'll always be a part of my vision.

Dancing in the wet grass,

Heels in our hands;

Underneath the stadium lights,

I'd rather prom in the rain with you,

Than a million perfect nights with a stranger.

Prom in the rain with you,

Forever.".

The crowd was going wild, Reese, Leo, and Bry's shouts of support could be heard above all the noise; people were up dancing, Brylee teared up mid song, even the vice principal was clapping. Quinn was sweating, her hair was out of place, her cap got thrown into the crowd at some point, and she was ecstatic; this was her favorite performance yet.

"Congratulations Quinn on becoming—

Q interrupted the VP as he walked toward her with her diploma in hand.

"Actually, Sir, I'm not done.", *Quinn interjected.*

"Oh.. okay, please, continue.", *Vice Principal Peters hesitantly permitted.*

"Great!", *she walked in front of the podium,* "Brylee Brown, will you please join me up here?".

The boys started smiling at Bry and encouraging her to get up on the stage; but, she stayed seated, frozen in shock.

"B, please, I don't know how much longer he's gonna let me have this mic.", *Quinn quipped.*

"Not much longer.", *Peters chimed in, leaning into the microphone.*

"See!", *Q locked eyes with her.*

Brylee, slightly embarrassed, got up and made her way toward the stage; Mr. Peters helped her up, and she joined her best friend. While Quinn was chill, cool, and collected, Bry was hot, nervous, and blushing.

"Thank you for joining me, Ms. Brown.", *Q confidently and playfully remarked as she moved the mic toward her friend's mouth, expecting a response.*

"Uhm..", *she nervously chuckled as she glanced at the crowd,* "You're welcome.".

"Now..", *Quinn turned toward the the audience,* "I know I already sang a song, but, doesn't the valedictorian usually give a speech??".

"YESSSS!!!! SPEECH! WOOOOOH!", *the students screamed and whistled.*

"Awesome.", *Q nodded as she took her place behind the podium.*

Bry just stood there, off to the side, awkward and unsure of what she was doing on stage.

"Boys!", *Quinn spoke to Leo and Reese,* "You recording? You're gonna wanna get this.".

They both had their phones up, in recording position, and gave her a reassuring thumbs up.

"Cool. I'll begin.", *Quinn continued,* "I've been elected this year's valedictorian, by default. That's right, I was a runner up, but, someone else rightfully took first place. That title was wrongly stolen from her, because of a stupid grudge.".

"BOOOOO!", *the crowd roared.*

"I know.", *she nodded,* "Totally unfair. So, who is the rightful valedictorian, you might ask? It's Ms. Brylee Brown!".

Q took her valedictorian mantle off, walked over to Brylee, placed it on her shoulders, then gave her a hug. During this exchange, the vice principal tried interrupting and stopping Quinn, but, the crowd defended her, and and caused Peters to back off. Q brought the mic to her lips once more, and faced the crowd, while holding her best friend's hand.

"Just to be clear, she may be valedictorian, but, I'm not done with my speech.", *Quinn began laughing with the crowd,* "This amazing woman is my best friend, and has been since the second grade—yes, the song was about us, but, most of you already know that. Why is she the real valedictorian? Because, not only does she excel at school, but, she excels at life. I don't know about you, but, I don't think that the honor of being valedictorian should be based solely on academics! What happens when you get into the real world, when you've been praised for your good grades, but your bad attitude was swept under the rug? What kind of adult does that create?! The decision should be based on the heart; that's the quality a leader should be recognized for… someone with a pure heart, a good heart. You shouldn't be awarded for the outward things that eventually fade away, but, for the inward things that stand the test of time. Eventually, grades don't matter, BUT, the heart ALWAYS matters! The valedictorian shouldn't be some kid who's test scores make the school's ratings go through the roof; it should be the person who lends a helping hand, always so selflessly, someone who leads by example everyday, someone who lovingly serves. So, class of 2021, let's hear it for the woman who checks all those boxes, MS. BRYLEEE HANNAHHH BROWNNNN!!!".

The crowd wildly exploded with cheers, shouts, and whistles. Brylee wiped the tears from her eyes, and let a smile grow on her face; as she embraced Quinn in a "thank you" hug, she felt 4 strong arms lift her into the air, which resulted in a tiny scream. It turned out to be Leo and Reese, they raced onto the stage in excitement, and put Bry on their shoulders like they do for the victor at the end of a baseball game. While they were celebrating, Mr. Peters came back onto the scene with a microphone.

"Okay, I understand that you guys are having a good time, but, I do have a graduation ceremony to put on.", *Peters continues,* "There is a schedule. Since you 4 took your chunk of time this way, I'll just hand you your diplomas while you're up here.".

The guys put Brylee down, and they all lined up, ready to receive what they'd been waiting for for 4 years. The sound guy started the grad music, the parents started recording a new video, and Mr. Peters had all of their diplomas in hand.

"Generally, I go in alphabetical order, but, in this…unique, circumstance, I'll go in the order by which you're standing.", *he explained,* "Reese, step up, please.".

Reese stepped forward, received his diploma, and shook the vice principal's hand.

"Leo…".

This continued with Quinn and Brylee until they all exited the stage; once they left, Mr. Peters quickly carried on, calling up the rest of the students. While he continued the ceremony, the kids intended to meet their parents, but, only KaraLee was sitting there, she was obviously the designated videographer.

"Where is everyone?", *Quinn asked her.*

"Yeah, where's dad??", *Bry joined.*

KaraLee didn't answer their questions, instead, she stood up and gave each and every one of them a hug.

"I'm so proud of each and everyone of you.", *Kara smiled at them,* "The ones I've known since birth, the ones I've known for years, and the ones I've known for weeks. I love all of you so much, I want you, ALL of you to know that.", *she looked first into the girl's eyes, then into the boys.*

Their hearts melted as she mothered them all.

"Well..", *Leo chuckled and wiped his eyes,* "I didn't actually think I was gonna cry today, here at least.".

KaraLee had "Aweeee" written all over her face, Quinn and Reese were laughing, and Bry giggled as she placed her hand on Leo's shoulder. Suddenly, Bryan ran toward them with urgency in his tone.

"Dad, hi! Where—

He cut Brylee off.

"Come quick! The parking lot!", *he was out of breath from running, and was resting his hands on his knees,* "Kim. Daniel! Come quick!".

The crew quickly, and nervously followed him into the parking lot; a thousand thoughts raced through their minds, they were trying to use positive thinking to push out the worst possible scenarios. They speedily approached the parking lot, only to find Daniel and Kim standing there, perfectly healthy, and smiling. As the kids looked around, they found 2 more smiles, one painted on Bryan's face, and one decorating KaraLee's.

"What is going on here?!", *Quinn exclaimed,* "You threw everyone into a panic, and now, you're smiling?! Y'all are creepy! In case you didn't know, senior pranks ended like last week!".

She was clearly shaken up, Reese took one of her hands while Bry took the other.

"I'm sure there's an explanation.", *Reese reasoned, trying to calm her down.*

"Quick!", *KaraLee shrieked,* "Behind you!".

"Nice, try, mom, I'm not falling for that.", *Bry tilted her head with a dry look on her face.*

"Uh, B.", *Quinn said while looking behind her,* "Look behind you.".

"Honestly. Now you're in on this too?", *she replied, slightly annoyed at the bad jokes.*

She humored her friend and turned around to see something that could either stop your heart or speed it up; in Brylee's case, it did both. There Leo was, suit under his gown, down on one knee. She gasped in surprise, put her hands over her mouth, and teared up; both Quinn and KaraLee were recording this special moment. He had a ring box held up, and an emerald sparkling in the midday sunlight.

"Brylee…", *he started with a confident smile,* "I believe that waiting is essential, in so many areas, how can you be sure that you're getting the very best if you don't wait at least a short amount of time? I mean, truly, they say, 'good things come to those who wait'. Well, I've waited, I've waited, and waited, and the good thing came to me. That's you, Love. The time to wait is over, I know that you're the one for me, so, as we enter into a new phase of life, why would I want to wait to start it with you? I want to start my life with you, Brylee. Will you say yes to beginning every day, for the rest of forever with me? Living it through with me, and ending it with me as well?", *his eyes were full of hope and happy tears.*

Brylee just stared for a second, feeling like she was in a dream. She looked toward her parents to see them excitedly nodding in approval, then toward Quinn, who was smiling and pretending not to cry; seeing everybody in support of her only confirmed what she already knew.

"Yes, Leo! Of Course! I feel the same way!", *she ran to him as he stood up, and smothered him with her hug.*

He laughed in relief as he embraced her, then momentarily pulled away so he could put the ring on her finger.

"Does it fit? Do you like it?", *Leo asked.*

"It's perfect. Did Quinn help you?", *she giggled.*

"As a matter of fact, it was your mom.", *he replied.*

"Didn't think I could keep the secret, huh?", *Quinn teased as she stopped her video.*

"No, it wasn't that; I asked him not to.", *Reese chimed in.*

"What? Why?", *Q asked, slightly confused as she turned to face him.*

She nearly fell back when she saw him, it was all like a dreamy flash.

"Pinch me.", *she said, slightly dazed.*

"Ow!", *she grabbed her arm.*

"You're welcome.", *Bry poked as she began recording.*

There was Reese, down on one knee just like Leo was a few moments ago. It didn't even feel real, the girls had always dreamed of getting engaged on the same day, (NEVER joint weddings though, to be perfectly clear), but this, this was a bestie fantasy come alive! Reese was teary eyed, his dark hair glistening in the sun, but not nearly as bright as the sapphire he was offering her; however, none of that sparkle came close to the dazzle of his smile. As Quinn came closer to him, he started speaking from his heart.

"Quinn, or, should I say, Q-Tip..", *he started,* "By the world's standards, we haven't known each other long, but, by the standard of my heart and soul, I've known you since my very beginning.. and I wanna know you till my very end. You're not at all who I thought you would be, and I mean that in the best way. I had a beautiful image of you pasted to my thoughts, and somehow, you far exceeded my expectation. I've come to know you, and every unique part of your family; every inch of your life, dark and light, and I'm here to stay. I'm all in, Quinn. I love you for you, and I want to grow with you and continue to fall in love with every version of you that's born year after year. I want all the stages of life with you. So, what I'm asking is, are you ready to let me be part of your everything else, now? I said I wanted a promise, that you'd be my date at prom, my girlfriend at graduation, and my wife for everything after. Can everything after start now?".

Quinn was beaming with excitement, and flooded with emotion; she didn't bother looking at anyone for approval, she knew that he was hers, and that was forever.

"Yes!", *she dropped to her knees and threw herself on him in a hug, nearly knocking him over,* "Everything after starts now!".

She kissed him on the cheek, and smiled into his eyes; as they were sitting there on the asphalt, he took her hand and slid the ring onto her finger.

"It fits right?", *he asked with a smile.*

"Brylee?", *she inquired.*

"Bryan, actually.", *he replied as he helped her off the ground.*

"What? Didn't trust me not to tell her?", *Bry joked.*

"Actually..", *Leo pulled her in for a kiss,* "I asked him not to.".

So, what happened after that, right? I mean, that's what I'd be wondering. Well, we got home that night and saw a giant tour bus in our driveway, I guess our question was answered. Dad said we could go on tour as long as me, Q, and the guys could show him that we could confidently drive that thing before the tour started. After a pretty short conversation, we decided we didn't want to tour until after our weddings, Mr. Walker agreed and allowed Quinn the fall tour slot. Oops, guess that means no fall enrollment, oh well. We decided that there was really no point to wait to get married, so, our wedding dates are set for each of our 18th birthdays, thankfully, our birthdays come after the boys, so, we'll all be ready.

Everyone is pretty happy about this, even Quinn's donors, *cough* sorry, I mean, PARENTS, are happy. Her dad's take on it? "If she won't be a doctor, at least she'll be a successful wife!", isn't that supportive! Well, I mean, close enough. Oh! Remember back when I said that I was gonna publish our adventures into like a book or.. make a show or something? Well, I've figured it out! I'm going to start an on tour vlog, "Quinn and Brylee: On Tour"! Eh, I'm still working on the name, but, you get the idea! Thankfully, Quinn and Reese won't be the only ones getting paid on this trip, it just so *happens, Leo can take his career on wheels.. and I think our vlog is gonna go viral, which means, you get paid!*

You know, when I started this year, I only had one thing on my mind, prom, but, I've learned that sometimes prom in the rain is better. What do I mean by that? Well, sometimes holding onto control and your own plans doesn't go so smoothly, sometimes when you let go, take off your heels and dance in the wet grass, things go way better.. better than you could imagine. OOH! I've got the name! I gotta tell Quinn!!

"Q!".

"Yeah?".

"I've got the name for the vlog!".

"Finally, cuz, "Quinn and Brylee: On Tour", definitely wasn't cutting it.".

"I know, I know! Ready?".

Quinn nodded in anticipation.

"Prom in the rain!", *Bry excitedly exclaimed.*

"It's perfect.", *Quinn replied with a smile.*

"I know.", *Brylee smiled, exhaled, and closed her eyes.*

ABOUT MATTISYN ELIZABETH

Mattisyn Elizabeth is an author, creative, and revelator.
She is 100% Holy Spirit lead, and has been anointed to reveal Abba's true heart to the world, in every avenue and adventure.
As a self-professed wildflower who lives life to the fullest and loves unapologetically, Mattisyn believes that clean and pure entertainment does not have to be, and SHOULD NEVER BE cheesy!
The misconception is that Heavenly ideas are the boring ones. She is confident that while reading her books, you'll quickly see that Heaven's creativity is the most colorful, wild, and explosive you'll ever experience, (Abba IS The Creator of fun!).

She is currently waiting for God's best. When she's not writing, you can find her laughing with her family or taking family recipes to "flavor town."

Made in the USA
Las Vegas, NV
21 July 2023